VOICES IN THE WOOD
And other tales

By Jan Foster-Bartlett

Hope you enjoy a few spooky tales.

Jan x

These stories are entirely a work of fiction. The names, characters and incidents portrayed in them are the work of the author's imagination. Any resemblance to actual persons, living or dead, events or localities is entirely coincidental.

Copyright © Jan Foster-Bartlett 2018

The right of Jan Foster-Bartlett to be identified as the author of this work has been asserted by her in accordance with the Copyright, Designs and Patents Act 1988

All rights reserved. No part of this publication may be reproduced, stored or introduced into a retrieval system, or transmitted, in any form, or by any means (electronic, mechanical, photocopying, recording or otherwise) without the prior written permission of the author.

For Miss Crabble who nurtured my love of English

Polly Payne	page 1
The Broch	page 11
Through the thin veil of time	page 16
A moment in time	page 19
The Bomber	page 36
The Bomber's tale	page 39
Tudor Banquet	page 41
Voices in the wood	page 46
Silence in library	page 56
The Legacy	page 59
Isobel	page 71
A different time, a different place	page 77
Be careful what you wish for	page 82
The other woman	page 86
Bluebell Wood	page 92
Inconvenient truth	page 98
The Black Horse ghost	page 102
The Forest incident	page 107
Heat	page 116
The whispering wood	page 118
The Bone Mill	page 123

Polly Payne

I first met her one spring day when the air was full of the sweet scent of bluebells and the sparkling water of the brook gurgled its path through the wood. I'd been fishing for sticklebacks when I heard a crackle of twigs behind me. I kept still and listened. I had my London wits about me and knew how to look after myself. I could sense someone close by and turning quickly I saw her, standing there in her long grey dress, looking at me, smiling.

She was the most beautiful person I had ever seen. Curls of ebony hair framed her porcelain white face. She had no lines of worry or frowns and her huge brown eyes looked kindly at me as she spoke in a soft voice.

'Hello Sammy. I hoped I would get to meet you soon.'

'How do you know my name?' I whispered back, feeling as if I was in a dream.

She laughed, 'I know about most people here young Sammy. Do you like living here? Is it nicer than London?'

I shrugged my shoulders, suddenly reminded of my old home and friends. If I still lived there I would have been chasing around, playing ball with Jack and Mickey, having fun. So, I mumbled into my chest, 'It's alright, I suppose.'

'Well don't you fret my boy, you will soon realise what a wonderful place this is. That's if you will let me show you,' she nodded and smiled, holding out her hand. I went willingly with her as she led me through the woods and we headed up the hill.

Our feet brushed past the flowers carpeting the woodland floor. The soft breeze whispered on the sunlit leaves and sent out ripples across the sea of blue around us. It was a heavenly day, so different from when Ma and I had first arrived at Stratton.

We had alighted the train at Godstone on a cold autumnal morning and we waited for the cart to take us and our few belongings to our new home. I wriggled as Ma rubbed at the soot that had speckled my face with black freckles as it had fluttered in through the window on our journey to Surrey. A bumpy ride northwards took us along a narrow dirt track framed by fields and hedgerows. I sat unusually quiet as we travelled past the few houses and farmsteads that were scattered here and there on our short trip. I had never seen so much greenery.

Our new home was amongst a small group of ancient cottages that sat at the base of the hill at the edge of the woods. We had replaced the dark smoky air of London with skies that seemed to be the colour of blood and sand. I soon realised it wasn't the sky I was seeing, but a forest so huge with the tallest of trees I had ever witnessed in my short life. I'd never seen so many, all so different and they all seemed to be swaying and rocking trying to lean towards me, as if they were hoping to hit me in the face.

'Go home, city boy. We don't want your sort here,' their words screamed in the wind, as gusts of orange leaves flew across my head like a flock of finches. Not that I knew about finches then, that was to come later, when I met Polly.

I would have preferred to live up in the village; it was too quiet where we were. I didn't like it much then. I didn't want to live there. In fact, I'd decided well before we moved I was going to hate it. I didn't want to leave my friends and move to the countryside. I was determined I wasn't going to like it. But Ma had thought it would be a new start for us. It was time she moved on she said. Five years since my Pa had been taken from us.

Our cottage was small, but as it was attached both sides it was cosy and I don't think I ever felt very cold living there. Not like our old place in London, where the windows rattled and as we had trouble finding fuel for the fire it was always freezing in the winter. The rats came and poked their noses under the door but usually left us in peace, it was probably too chilly for them too. But at Stratton it felt clean and secure and even though I said I hated it, to be honest deep down I knew it was safe and the best thing we'd ever done. But I wasn't going to admit that to Ma.

She tried to keep on the good side of the people from the big house. She worked up there doing the laundry and told me she needed to work hard and not upset them else we'd be out on our ears. She'd smile and chat to Mr Hawkins when he rode by with his pack of dogs yelping and barking. He was the man who looked after the hounds up at the house for the local hunt. I would scowl at him for I knew what he did with those dogs. I hadn't known to begin with, being the town born lad that I was, but Polly told me all about the hunters.

That first day I met Polly had been the best day of my life. She opened a whole new world to me. She held my hand as we headed up the hill through the woods knowing the way even though there was no obvious path to me at the time, although now I could probably do the route blindfolded. We eventually came out into a clearing and that was when I first set eyes on her home.

It was more a shack than a house, put together in a rather haphazard way but it looked inviting with smoke billowing out of the roof and surrounded by beds of sweet smelling flowers and bushes. Chickens roamed freely, some scratching about in a huge pile of rotting vegetation near the edge of the enclosure. A pony snorted and shuffled his feet, as he stood tethered to a tree. And at the side of the cottage was the most brightly coloured contraption that I'd ever seen. It was red and gold with yellow swirls and big blue flowers painted on its side. Four huge wheels held it in place and jutting his head out of one of the windows was a little dog, his tongue hanging down as he looked across at me.

'What's that?' I asked, awe struck.

'That used to be my home Sammy, before I settled here. It would take me all over the country. My, I've seen some wonderful places in my life.'

The little dog started barking and twisted himself out through the window and came sprinting over to us, tail wagging with delight.

'Young Rascal likes you, I see. He approves of my new friend,' she picked up the dog and it wriggled with delight in her arms, licking her face and neck as she laughed.

She introduced me to all of the animals, speaking to them as if they understood. I had laughed at her and said as much.

'But of course they understand me Sammy. You will soon learn child, that all animals understand us, we can converse with them, you just have to take time to be still and listen.'

As well as the chickens, pony and Rascal the terrier she also had so many cats I cannot begin to tell you how many there were. The numbers seemed to change each day. They were everywhere, black, tabby, white, all colours and shapes, all so happy living with Polly. The cats never seemed to trouble the chickens or the other small birds that Polly had in her home. She would nurse any injured bird back to health. They seemed to know she was able to help them and somehow in their distress, managed to make their way to her home, so she could take them in and heal their fractured wings or let them rest a while before letting them fly off into the wood, healed and happy.

I began visiting Polly on my way home from school. I hated the days Ma asked me to call into the village for provisions after my lessons as it meant I didn't have time to see Polly too. I much preferred my lessons with her, teaching me about the trees and the wild flowers, their names and how they could be used to heal people's ailments. School seemed boring in comparison.

Don't get me wrong, it was good to go to school and after I had proved myself with the local boys that I could hold my own in a fight, they accepted me, sometime laughing at my accent but I did make some friends but none of them as special as Polly Payne. Although she never said as much, I felt it was best to keep our friendship a secret and this I managed to do until the day I was with her in the woods, helping her to gather wild sorrel to add to the pot of soup she was making. The wild garlic growing by the brook was coming to an end but it still sent up wafts of its delicious aroma. I'd called across to Polly who was rummaging about under a tree, digging up a root of some sort.

'Polly, shall I get you some Ramsons?'

'Thank you but no Sammy, they are past their best now child.'

The joy of that day was soon brought to an end when I heard my mother's voice bellow, 'Samuel Lewis, get here this minute!'

I could see her near the foot of the hill, through the cover of the trees that were just beginning to fill out with lush new summer growth. Her arms placed on her hips in the pose I recognised that meant I was in her bad books.

'You best go Sammy,' Polly quietly called to me.

'I'll see you soon Polly.' I called back as I sped down the gritty woodland path towards my angry mother.

'What are you doing with that old hag Sammy?' she tugged at my arm roughly, pulling me down the last few feet of the steep path.

'What old hag? I was only helping Polly find some greens for her cooking pot. I like her. She's nice.'

Ma yanked me along the lane toward our cottage, 'Not what I've heard Sam. You keep away from Polly Payne, you 'ear? The folk round 'ere don't like her sort. You mind out boy or she'll be putting you in her ruddy pot!'

Well, although I'd had an inner sense that Ma would think Polly should be out of bounds, I really couldn't understand why people didn't like her. She was the only person here I really liked.

'Why's that Ma? I think she's kind.'

She cuffed my ear, 'Kind? You keep away from that old woman; do you hear me?'

'She ain't old Ma. She's really pretty and she's much younger than you!' and with that I got another swipe.

'You just do as your mother says Samuel.' was the only reply I got.

I began asking a few of my new pals at school about Polly. It was odd, for they all said how old and wrinkly she was and how she was scary up there in the woods with her animals. I didn't argue with them but I knew they were wrong. She was kind and sweet and her face wasn't wrinkly at all. She looked much younger than Ma. I let my visits stop for a while until I felt Ma had forgotten all about her and then began venturing up the hillside again to help Polly with her foraging and caring for the creatures.

It was one early spring day that I arrived at her house and although the fire was crackling and inviting, there was no sign of Polly. I called out and Rascal came running across, tail held high, leaping up to me with delight.

'Well young chap, where's your mistress?'

He jumped up, front paws on my shins and I bent and picked him up and gave him a cuddle.

'Where is she then boy?'

Polly had taught me how to listen, hear the messages that nature gave us. I stood quietly with Rascal in my arms and let my head tune into the surroundings. I could tell Rascal was beginning to sense my feelings and struggled to get down. He began to run through the trees, up the hill to the big field, stopping and looking back at me every so often to be sure I was following.

The field was furrowed deeply from the recent ploughing, the soil dark and rich and I savoured the earthy smell that filled my nostrils. Polly had shown me over the years to appreciate these wonderful smells of nature. I saw movement in the field ahead and stood and watched with delight as a drove of hares ran and darted about ahead of me. Rascal had left my side and I was pulled from my hare watching when I heard him begin to whine. He was sitting at the edge of the field, his paw patting at something he had found.

'What is it boy?' I looked down and flinched when I looked into the eyes of a hare that had its back leg caught in a trap.

'Oh, you poor thing!' I knelt down and with all my might managed to carefully pull the offending trap open and scoop the hare into my arms. I ran down the path back to Polly's shack and lay the hare onto one of the cat's beds and began to mix up various herbs as Polly had shown me, ready to soothe its injury. Fortunately, its wound didn't look too deep and after bathing it well with some warm salt water I gently smoothed a little of the salve over its leg. Its huge eyes never left my face all the time I tended the beautiful creature.

I continued to care for it and all this time there was no sign of Polly, so I would creep out of my house early in the morning and again in the evening so I could feed and water all the animals and keep an eye on the place for Polly until she returned, which I just knew in my heart that she would. Within a week, the hare was looking much better and as I headed off for school, pleased with my administrations, I knew it would soon be able to fend for itself again.

That evening as I made my way up through the woods I heard a voice I recognised. It was Polly! I ran up the path and there she was, sitting outside the shack getting the last of the evening sun.

'Polly, you're back! I am so pleased to see you. I've been worried. Where have you been?'

She looked tired and didn't look as bright as she usually did.

'I'm fine boy, just not been myself this past week so, had to keep out of the way until I felt a bit better.'

'Oh Polly. You could have stayed here. I would have looked after you. I was here every day anyway, tending an injured hare. I wish I could become a doctor or a vet when I am older.'

'You can do anything you want to boy. If you *really* wish it, you can become whatever you want to be.'

'I loved helping the hare Polly. Have you seen it? It's inside resting in one of the cat's beds,' I put my head round the door but it was gone.

'You did a grand job there Sam. The hare has left now, almost good as new. Come on, let's have a brew,' she stood up and I followed her, noticing she hobbled slightly as she made her way back into her house.

'But you've hurt your leg too Polly! Can I help you?'

She smiled at me and patted my arm, 'You've already done that young Sam, thank you'.

I looked at her questioningly but she held up her hand, 'Ask me no questions and I'll tell ye no lies. Come, sit down, let's have a nice nettle tea.'

Life carried on and summer came and went and autumn passed us by gently that year. Ma still worked at the big house, she worked hard and looked tired most evenings so I would help out as much as I could at home. I think it was because of this that she didn't object when I brought home one of Polly's kittens to live with us. He was a cute little black cat and I named him Mickey after my old school pal from London. He'd sleep down in the kitchen in front of range during the day and at night he'd disappear, probably having fun hunting for mice.

It was a pity that he wasn't sleeping in front of the range that January day when the hunt and the hounds came clambering along the lane chasing the scraggy fox that darted across the brook into our garden. The noise of the hounds was bedlam as they ran in a frenzy after their prey. Mickey had been seriously studying a vole he had seen by the waterside and fortunately I spotted him in time just as the hound headed towards him, eager to feed its blood lust.

I picked Mickey up and kicked out at the dog. I tried not to be too vicious, as I knew that they were only doing what they had been trained to do. It wasn't their fault that the stupid men found glory in hurting innocent animals.

'Get away, go on shoooo,' I kicked again and then looked up to see Mr Hawkins astride his horse looking down at me, rage in his eyes.

'Stop kicking my hound boy,' he spat at me with venom.

His horse reared up and I narrowly missed being caught in the face with a hoof. Ma had heard the commotion and had come running outside just as Mr Hawkins had unleashed his whip and she caught the full impact as he splayed the snake like weapon towards me.

'Ma, Ma!' I dropped Mickey and he ran off into the undergrowth as I went to Ma's aid.

She had fainted with the shock and was lying on the ground, the material on her dress ripped, where the whip had cut through to her skin. I fell to the ground and sat holding her to me, looking up at Mr Hawkins.

'What have you done? You are an evil man. I hate you!'

He spat on the ground next to me, 'You're just scum!' and with that pulled at the reins and rode off.

The sounds of the hooves vanished into the distance as I sat stroking Ma's head wondering what to do. I wasn't strong enough to pick her up and take her inside. I needed help. But someone was watching over us that day as I heard footsteps along the gravel path and will admit I shed tears of relief when I saw that it was Polly.

'Young Mickey came up to see me, so I knew something was wrong. Looks like you need some help there, young Sam,' she knelt down and rubbed my back, 'Come now, let's get your Ma inside.'

It took a good few weeks to get Ma feeling well again, the whip had cut deeply into her flesh. The few weeks before the accident she had been working extra hard up at the house as they'd had lots of guest over Christmas. She was already worn out and run down so the whipping was the final straw for my poor Ma.

But she healed quickly with Polly's help. She had shown me a good combination of herbs to help beat the infection. She stayed overnight with us until she was sure Ma had broken her fever. She came down from her shack most days to sit with Ma, who now realised that Polly wasn't the evil witch everyone had branded her, but just a kindly woman with a great knowledge of healing and an amazing connection with animals.

It had been while Polly had been upstairs sitting with Ma that Mrs Evelyn from the big house arrived at our cottage. I watched from the window as her driver helped her down from the pony and trap and followed her to our door carrying a big parcel of food.

If she felt out of place in such a humble abode she didn't show it. She was kindness itself.

'We heard all about your mother and the terrible accident that happened. Mr Hawkins has been heavy handed too many times of late and now, this latest incident – well - he just went too far. My husband felt it his duty to dismiss him.'

She ventured further into the cottage and sat down on the bench by the range and held out her hands to the warmth. Her eyes took in her surrounding and finally rested on me.

'You tell your mother not to worry, her job is safe until she is well enough to return to work. And how about you? How are you getting on? I hear from the school master that you are a bright lad and doing well with your lessons.'

I finally found my voice, 'Yes Ma'm. I want to be a doctor one day.'

'Really? Is that so? Well, we will need a good doctor in the village. Old Dr Marshall can't go on forever and when he gives up he can begin to enjoy some leisure time while he is able.

We must encourage you with your lessons young man, maybe you should come and borrow some books from our library to help with your studies.'

'Well thank you, I would like that very much Mrs Evelyn,' I managed to reply, totally amazed.

With my keen sense of hearing I caught a shuffling noise and watched as a creature scampered down the stairs and out of the door. Glancing out of the window, I watched as the hare caught my eye before darting up through the woods. Polly's words came back to me. If you really wish it, you can become whatever you want to be.

The Broch

She looked out of the window; it was already starting to get dark. She wasn't happy making the journey this late in the day but he had sounded so insistent. Grabbing her waterproof jacket from the hall she braved the elements and shut the front door behind her. She looked back wistfully at the warm glow of the light in the sitting room through the gap in the curtains. Leaving the image of the cosy room behind, she darted down the steps to the road and to her car.

As the hot air blasted out from the vents, the windscreen slowly cleared to reveal the way ahead and she reluctantly pulled out of her parking bay. The drizzle was turning into a mist and the streetlights hardly illuminated the stone of the grey buildings that edged the road. She stopped at the T-junction and wiped the remaining moisture from the windscreen. Indicating right, she took the Dunvegan Road and headed west out of town.

The landscape opened out ahead and she soon left the damp evening gloom of Portree behind. Small pockets of mist whispered along the route but it wasn't long before the road ahead shrunk away from view, as the low cloud grew heavier and descended into a thick fog, shrouding the car from the outside world. Maria's fingers gripped the steering wheel tightly as she drove the miles to Dunvegan, wishing she was back home.

Michael had been so keen for her to see the find he'd uncovered at the Iron Age broch. Why it couldn't wait until he returned in a few days she didn't know. He wasn't even letting on what he had found but was really insistent that she went over that day. She leant forward and peered into the swirling gloom, checking she hadn't missed her turning.

The few lights at Dunvegan gave her brief respite from the poor visibility and she glanced across in envy at a couple heading into the inviting looking pub. She took the road southwards and along the route a scattering of white stone cottages hinted at their presence through the fog. As she finally approached her destination, the mists started to lift and in the western skies the weak rays of the setting sun started to filter through the clouds. Maria pulled into the lay-by at the side of the road and jumped down onto the grassy bank that led down to the rocky shoreline. On the other side of the road, the land rose steeply heavenward, crowned with the ruined broch. She looked up and spotted Michael's figure moving on the mountainside. She waved but he was engrossed in his work and didn't see her.

She began the trek across the boggy ground to the base of the ruin and made her way up over the rocks and boulders. When she finally reached the top, she found Michael kneeling at the edge of a jumble of stones of an ancient wall.

Maria crouched down next to him, 'So what was so important I had to journey out in this foul weather?'

He turned and smiled, eyes alight with excitement, 'I've found a grave! See there,' he indicated with his trowel to a hint of bone beneath the soil, 'Looks like a skull. I've got a good feeling about this Maria. He has been waiting a long time for me to find him.'

She observed him at work while he continued brushing at the soil, as he began the painstaking task of uncovering the remains. She was always enthralled when she watched him work and was amazed how easily he had mastered the task with his disability. He had told her that his injury was the result of an accident a long time ago, he would never say more and she never pushed him for details. She watched as his misshapen right hand, with its remaining two fingers worked skilfully, as he caressed his find.

'That's amazing Michael. Have you found anything else?'

'No - not yet. I'm hoping there will be some grave goods. Something he took with him to the afterlife.'

They had spent some time together absorbed in the find when Maria looked down in the direction the road. The fog had curled its tongue over the land once more, lapping up all that it touched and her car and the road were now hidden from view.

'I better get moving. I'll ring the uni for you as soon as I can, see if I can get someone down here to help you lift the skeleton.'

Michael started covering up the grave with tarpaulin, 'Okay, I'll call it a day now. I've got my tent set up round the back of the broch. I'll be dead to the world long before you climb into your bed.'

'It's a pity my sister is coming to stay for a few days, otherwise I could have stayed and helped. I'll come back once she's gone.'

'Don't worry. I'll be fine.'

She kissed him on the cheek, 'Be mindful of the spirits - don't go upsetting the ancients!'

He looked at her with a hint of sadness in his eyes, 'Maria, I know I haven't always shown it, but you do know that all the time we have been together I have loved you. Don't you?'

She smiled, 'Of course I do and I love you.' As she began the descent to her car she turned and called up, 'I'll let you know when the uni can send some help,' but her voice was lost in the wind and swirling cloud.

Next morning Maria rang the professor and arranged for two field workers to be sent along to assist the dig. She rang Michael's mobile but there was no response. Probably still tucked up in his sleeping bag she thought, as she began getting the place ready for her sister's visit. She needed to have a tidy up and get the spare room ready, Beth hadn't been to stay for a long while, she was really looking forward to seeing her. It was a pity she wouldn't get a chance to meet Michael at last. He always seemed to be away when she came over from the mainland to see her.

'I'm beginning to wonder if he really exists!' Beth had joked when she had seen her the previous month. Maria had taken a trip up to Inverness for supplies and Beth had invited her to stay overnight.

'I made up the double, I assumed you would come with Michael.'

Maria had shaken her head and made his apologises. He had a report he had to get finished, she had told her. She knew he wasn't good with people. Well, not living people anyway. He was at his happiest when he was surrounded by bones or remnants of the past. He hated the trappings of modern living. She was sure he would step back in time if he could.

She had tried to persuade him a number of times to meet Beth or go with her when she went away for weekends to see some of her old uni friends but he would just smile and tell her that she was all he wanted. She knew that wasn't true, he would be just as happy without her, she was sure of that.

It was a few days later when she was waving Beth goodbye when the phone rang.

'Hi Maria?' said a voice she didn't recognise.

'Yes, who is this?'

'My name is Barry Green...from the archaeology dept. I work with Professor Gordon. I've been sent up with a colleague to help with the broch dig.'

She put the phone to her other ear and moved over to the window seat and watched as her sister's car disappeared from view, 'Oh good. You've arrived. How's it going? I haven't spoken to Michael since Friday. '

'Well, we have been here since yesterday but there is no sign of Michael.'

Her muscles tensed, 'Are you sure? I can't believe he would leave the dig unattended.'

She jumped up and began to pace the room. What was going on? Where was he? Dammit! She should have tried ringing him again.

'But he must be there, he was camped behind the broch. Are you there now?' she asked.

'Yes, we both plan on staying put here for the rest of the day, if you would like to come over?'

It was forty-five minutes later when she arrived back at the broch. It looked so different. No fog today. There was glorious sunshine with clear skies. The broch was visible in all its ruined glory as it watched over the shimmering sea. A youngish man with long hair pulled back into a ponytail came running down, taking the rocky hill like a mountain goat.

'Maria, Hi, I'm Barry. Thanks for coming over. We've found evidence of the grave that Michael had uncovered. My colleague is up there now checking it out.'

'And Michael?' Maria asked, as she followed the young man up the hillside, her stomach tight with concern.

'No sign at all I'm afraid.'

As they reached the hilltop, his colleague stood up and rubbed his fingers clean on his trousers before shaking Maria's hand.

'Hi, I can see why Michael was so excited about this grave, it's fascinating! So far I've only uncovered part of the skeleton - an arm and hand. Really interesting and unusual. The hand is rather deformed and only has two fingers.'

Through the Thin Veil of Time

The eerie tower of the Central London District school building shines out and can be seen glowing for miles, but the clock stopped long ago. Maybe they cannot find any one brave enough to face the ghosts that are said to haunt the long winding climb up to the top.

I look out from the upstairs window of room six and see her walking up the long driveway towards the gates. An avenue of horse chestnut trees tower around her, guiding her route. This building has played its part in so many lives. Poor, destitute and orphaned young children once walked through those gates. Their journey beginning in the dark and depressing streets of London before they were whisked away into an alien world of fields, trees and sky. As they travelled up the long driveway, their apprehension surely grew. Reaching the top of the chestnut drive they faced a towering grey construction looming ahead. How did they feel when they arrived? Was it a sense of freedom from squalor or was it imprisonment?

Now the building is the community centre for the local housing estate. How many of its visitors know of its history? The girl walking up the driveway knows. I could tell she would understand its layers of history when I first saw her. I knew she could feel other lives resonating within the fabric of the building. As a small baby, she was brought along here for her immunisations and I saw her eyes find mine. There was knowledge in her, even then. She felt the power of the building.

I have followed her life closely and watched her as she interacted with the place. At the age of ten I saw her on Saturday mornings, running and giggling as she darted up the stairs and along the dark corridors to the hall where the film shows were shown for the local children. They chuckled and cried out as the screen displayed the antics of the Keystone cops and Laurel and Hardy. The big hall was full of laughter, noise and shouting. Little did they know when they sat and laughed as Charlie Chaplin played the fool, that as a child he had actually sat in the same hall with other pupils, all sitting in long rows and eating their meals in silence. Be seen and not heard was the order of the day. Not the case in this new modern world.

I observed the girl at age twelve when she would arrive every week wearing her smart St John ambulance uniform and learn how to mend the sick and she would practise how to bind up injuries.

She has been venturing to and fro here all of her young life. Now she is in her teenage years and I watch her as she approaches the building. She is now coming to attend her dancing lessons. It is a good place to be with friends on a Saturday morning. Teenagers being kept off the street, kept on the straight and narrow. No different from all the youngsters who were schooled here in Victorian times until the 1930s. The memories of those who were here before are concealed within the building, they hide in the walls, waiting for someone to wake them from their slumbers.

The dancing class girl looks around her, she has been told many times the tales of the spirits that walk this grand old building. She has always been able to sense them. She doesn't know who the ghosts are. Are they the spirits of children who died in the infirmary here or are they ghosts of Victorian teachers who are still turning in their graves after hearing the likes of The Who and Deep Purple rehearsing here in the basement in the late 1960s?

As the young girl ventures in through the hallway, the building wraps its cloak around her. She moves along the corridors and then takes the stairs and rushes past the doorway that leads into the big hall. This was once the dining room of the school. Sometimes she is sure she hears the murmurs of voices and clatter of plates and cutlery. She takes the stairs quickly to room six. The famed room six. This is the room where she comes every week for her ballroom dancing lessons. It is said that it is the most haunted room in the building.

The girls from the dancing class always try visiting the Ladies room along the corridor in pairs. There is now a false wall just as you enter and they have been told that behind the wall is a blocked off staircase that leads down to where the old infirmary was once situated. In its time, it was a busy stairwell with nurses in starched aprons, white bonnets and long grey frocks heading down to tend the sick young children. Some say that even now their footsteps can be heard from behind the panel. If they do feel brave enough to visit the cloakroom alone, the girls make sure they get out of there as soon as possible. It makes me smile when I see them darting out as quick as they can. That's it - run along the corridor back to the class. How they love to be scared!

    I look across at the girl, she is concentrating hard as she practises her dance steps. She looks up, suddenly aware of my presence and smiles at me. There is just a thin veil of time that separates us. I leave her dancing and set off back along the corridor. I straighten my starched apron and adjust my bonnet and head towards the dining room for my luncheon but first I will head down the staircase and call into the infirmary to check on my young patients.

A Moment in Time

'Do I know you?' Maisie asked, as the old woman settled herself into the chair, 'You look familiar.'

She took in the features of the wrinkled face, as the old lady's thin lips took a sip of tea. Her lower eyelids were heavy with the moisture that filled her milky grey eyes, her cheeks were crisscrossed with lines. She looks ancient, thought Maisie. The elderly woman's gnarled hands shook as she held onto the cup that commemorated a royal event. It was etched with gold swirls that reflected the sunlight into Maisie's eyes, making the old girl look almost transparent.

'Let me tell you about the events in this house, let me tell you my tale and then you can decide if you know me.'

Maisie was intrigued. What did the old girl have to tell her about the house? And either she knew her or she didn't. Why the cloak and dagger? She had hinted that something terrible had happened long ago. Maisie had her doubts, the old biddy was probably trying to put her off. The house was up for sale but maybe her children were making her sell. Putting her in a home maybe? She didn't want to move, so was putting off prospective buyers.

She picked up her cup and saucer and smiled at the old lady. She'd listen to her tale, but it wasn't going to put her off. She loved what she had seen of the house. It would suit them right down to the ground. Pete had told her to put in an offer if she was certain. He trusted her judgment and he'd back her all the way. Only another month and he'd be back in the country. She couldn't wait.

'It's just at the edge of Miltonshaw village Pete.' she had told him when he rang a few days before, 'Close enough to walk to the village shops, there's a village school too…so…if we do decide…'

He had laughed down the receiver, 'I think you have already decided Maisie! Sounds like you are going to be giving me a good welcome home.'

They had discussed having children a number of times. When his contract in Sydney had finished, he had told her, maybe then they could plan a family. But he had also told her that when he had been working out in L.A. and when he had been in Rotterdam. Still this time it would be different. He had taken a two year contract in Cambridge. She would see him every day, no long distance love anymore. Surely now was the time they could make the baby she had been wanting for the past ten years. She was thirty three. Her clock was ticking.

They'd been moved in two months, it had been a busy time of unpacking and decorating and Maisie took a rare moment to sit in the garden. There was a great deal that needed doing outside too. It was so overgrown with ivy trailing across the weed infested flower beds. The huge beech tree that sat behind the back fence had been shedding its leaves for many a year making the paths slippery and dangerous. She had great plans for the garden. Maisie smiled as a little flock of blue tits made their way across the shrubs, stopping at the bird feeder as they made their morning forage. The newly fledged birds waited, hopeful that their parents would feed them but it looked as if the mother had decided it was time they learnt to fend for themselves. It was a hard job for them, bringing up their young.

She wished she had a chance to know how it felt - to bring a new life into the world. Maybe this month she would get good news. How she would tell Peter when she did get pregnant she didn't know. How would he react?

That first night when they had moved into the house, feeling shattered from moving so many boxes and trying to unpack as much as they could, they had sat snuggled up together on the sofa before heading up to bed. Pete had sat with his arm around her shoulder, twisting her long auburn hair around his fingers. She sat back against his body feeling content. Finally, after years of renting, they had their own place, they were settled at last. They had survived the first fraught years of their relationship when he had left his wife and children for her. It hadn't been easy and his two boys hadn't spoken to their father for many years. It was only now with families of their own that they had thawed to their father's infidelity and the break-up of their home during their teenage years.

'Pete?' Maisie had dared herself to speak the words. 'Do you think the time is right now?'

She felt his body tense as he answered, 'Not babies again Maisie! We've only just moved in. Give me a chance!'

She twisted round and looked at him, held her hand up to his face. He looked pretty good for fifty three. She had never cared about the twenty year age difference between them. It had never seemed to matter. But now as her own biological clock ticked further into her thirties she knew time wasn't on their side.

'But darling, we can't wait forever. Don't you want us to have a child?'

He stroked her hair gently, 'Oh course I do. But let me settle into the new contract first. Let's get this place decorated and talk about it again then. Okay?' he planted a kiss on her nose and jumped up, putting out his hands to her, 'Come on, let's go to bed. I'm dead on my feet,' he glanced around at the boxes still to be unpacked, 'We've got another busy day tomorrow.'

She had followed him up the stairs. Her toiletries were still in a bag and she had taken it into the bathroom with her, located her toothbrush and began to clean her teeth. She glanced at her reflection in the mirror and for a brief second she thought of the old girl who had lived here before and the crazy things she had told her about the house. It was an unhappy house, she had told Maisie. Unhappy with its path. What on earth did she mean by that?

The old lady had shaken her head, 'I can't interfere. I can't tell you anymore. But promise me you will think hard before you make any major decisions for your life. You may not like the consequences. Make sure it really will make you happy. I didn't think. Don't make that mistake again.'

Maisie didn't have a clue what the woman's ramblings were about. That's all they had been, a demented old woman's ramblings.

After cleaning her teeth, she continued her nightly ritual and wiped the makeup from her face. Just one more thing to do before bed. She pulled out the packet from her bag and took out the pill for that day, about to place it on her tongue. She stopped and looked back at her reflection. She would be thirty four next birthday. She could hear Pete in the bedroom, he was fiddling with the radio, trying to tune it into a local station.

'Isn't she lovely' by Stevie Wonder began to play and she heard Pete singing along, probably unaware of the irony of his words, 'Isn't she precious? Less than one minute old, I never thought through love we'd be, making one as lovely as she.'

Maisie rolled the tiny pill around between her fingers deep in thought. Then, decision made, she flung it down the lavatory, flushed it out of sight and put the packet back into her toiletry bag.

A few weeks after moving in, Pete started his contract down at Cambridge. He had promised that the journey would be short enough for him to travel home every day but within a month he was ringing her to say he was booking into a hotel during the week. She tried to make out where he said he was staying but the hubbub of the pub from where he was ringing from made it difficult to make out his words. He'd be back on Friday he had told her, it would be great, they would spend weekends together.

So, Maisie did what she always had to do during her life as Peter's partner and carve out a life for herself whilst he was away. At their last home, she had joined various clubs, helped out at the church luncheon club. She made lots of friends and quite enjoyed herself but it all changed when Pete came back from his trips abroad. He didn't want her going out to her clubs and meeting up with her new friends when he was there. He wanted her to himself. She felt as if she lived a double life.

It was on a warm spring afternoon, a few days after Peter had headed off again to Cambridge for his week away that Maisie called into the nearest neighbour who lived just along the lane. Maisie had seen the blonde haired woman cycling by the house a few mornings in a row and earlier that day, as Maisie had been weeding the front border, the woman had waved as she pedalled by, calling out to her to pop in for a cuppa that afternoon.

She walked up the path and the front door swung open almost as soon as Maisie had rung the doorbell.

'Hello! So glad you could make it. Do come in,' her nearest neighbour's beaming smile greeted her at the door. At her feet, a small terrier sized dog jumped up at Maisie, delighted at the new smells from the visitor.

Irene Tanner bent down and picked up her dog, apologising for his behaviour, 'so sorry about Reggie, he will calm down in a moment. Do come in,' she made her way along the narrow dark hallway and opened a door to her right. Maisie followed, her eyes trying to make out the paintings that adorned the walls in the gloomy hall.

They walked into the bright sitting room. An old stone fireplace framed a wood-burning stove. It had been put to bed for the summer and now was adorned with a basket of dried flowers and lavender stalks.

'Hello neighbour,' Irene said and invited Maisie to sit in one of the large dumpy armchairs, 'I'm Irene by the way...Reggie you know,' she laughed.

Maisie held out her hand, 'Maisie. Nice to meet you.'

'So how are you enjoying living down the lane. Not too quiet for you?'

'No, not at all. It's nice to be near enough to the village but still have the peace here with the fields and footpaths so close by.'

Reggie jumped up onto Irene's lap and she began to scratch his head, 'Yes, good for dog walking. Do you have a dog?'

Maisie shook her head, 'No, no pets. Just me...well, me and Pete that is.' Crikey she had almost forgotten about him. She felt a pang of guilt and added, 'Pete works away a lot, so during the week it's just me.'

'Where does he work? I see him driving off in that swish car of his on a Sunday evening. I assume he has a long commute?'

Maisie sat forward in the chair and said, 'No, not as long as the last contract - he was working out in Sydney for six months, before that he was in L.A. for four months. This time he's not that far, just Cambridge.'

'Cambridge?' Irene frowned, 'but that isn't that far is it? Only about two hours if that. Couldn't he commute? Must be hard on you, him being away so much. What a pity you still have to be apart, especially with just moving into your new home. Do you work?'

Maisie looked down at her hands folded tightly on her lap, 'No I don't work,' but I would like to, she thought. Pete had felt it best that she didn't work, that way she could have the savings in her name, keep the taxman at bay. He'd told her it was a good idea otherwise they'd be paying top whack on his salary and more tax when they stashed it away. Up until the house purchase she'd had a tidy sum in her name, but now the savings were all but gone. Maybe she could get a little part time job now?

Irene headed off to the kitchen to make a coffee for them both and Maisie sat back in the lumpy but comfy chair and looked around the room. Either side of the fireplace shelves were laden with books. It looked as if they had been neatly stacked to begin with but now every new purchase had been wedged into gaps as best they could. The dried lavender sent up heavenly scent and Maisie found herself feeling calm and relaxed as she sat in the room.

The door suddenly burst open and Irene emerged carrying a tray with deliciously smelling coffee and hot cross buns laden with butter. Irene had sat opposite her and filled her in about the village, warned her to avoid the art group as it was just a place that the nosey old busy bodies met to get the local gossip. Maisie told her about the groups she had belonged to at the last place she had lived and what a friendly place it had been.

'Well hopefully you will think the same about Miltonshaw too,' Irene sat back in her chair and licked the last smear of butter from her fingers. She patted her stomach, 'Mmm, that was a nice treat. It's nice to indulge now and again. Mrs Coleman and I used to meet up for coffee once a week and usually treat ourselves to cake of some sort.'

'Mrs Coleman?' Maisie asked, popping the last piece of hot cross bun into her mouth.

'Yes, the lady who lived in your place. We used to have some laughs. In the summer, we'd sometimes head off down the lanes on our bikes and have a picnic. Some good spots round here.'

'Mrs Coleman? Who lived at our house...out on a bike? Really?' Maisie said, looking perplexed, 'was she the old girl's daughter? I just assumed she lived on her own.'

Old girl? No old lady lived in your house. It was Sue Coleman and her teenage son. They lived there...er...must be about ten years. It was Douglas and Annie Winters before that, probably in their forties when they sold up.'

'So, who on earth was the old woman I had a cup of tea with?'

Maisie asked a number of local people and nobody had any idea who the old lady had been, even the Estate Agents drew a blank. In the end she tried to forget about the strange woman and begun to get involved with the village. Soon she was living her double life again. Peter would come home on a Friday evening and they would spend two nights together. He was loving and attentive and they would spend Sunday mornings snuggled up in bed with the papers. They would cook and eat delicious meals together and sit outside sipping wine in the evening sunshine. Some days they would head out for walks along the local footpaths. One Sunday afternoon they bumped into Irene walking Reggie.

'Hiya you two. It's a great day for a walk, isn't it?' Irene had smiled and stopped hoping to chat.

'It sure is,' Pete had answered coldly and tugged on Maisie's hand for them to continue on their way. Maisie had looked back towards Irene and mouthed, 'Sorry'.

'Why did you have to be rude Pete? Irene's nice. I told you I go out for walks with her and little Reggie during the week. I was hoping you could get to know her, she is my friend after all.'

He had squeezed her hand tightly, a bit too tightly and turned to her.

'I didn't mean to seem rude, but she is your friend Maisie. Your friend for when I am away. But I am here now and it's my time.'

Her stomach tightened. She didn't like to upset him, for he was right, it was their time. Two nights a week was not long enough.

She had questioned him after dinner that evening about the journey, she'd looked it up on google and the AA site and both indicated the journey shouldn't take longer than an hour and half.

'Those sites don't take into account the commuter traffic. It takes me well over two hours. I need to be fresh and bright for my work, you wouldn't want me turning up at the start of my working day already tired out, would you? You don't want me to lose this job, do you? How would we eat and pay the bills?'

'No Peter, of course not. I'm sorry. Talking of jobs, I was wondering if now, as I don't hold much money in my name anymore, maybe now I could start looking for a job of my own.'

He slung down his knife and fork and looked at her with eyes she didn't recognise, 'Work? Why would you need to work? I can provide for both of us. Anyway,' he laughed, 'What would you do? It's been over ten years since you worked, things have moved on, everything is on computers now. You'd never cope.'

She had taken their empty plates through to the kitchen and flicked on the kettle, her eyes smarting with unshed tears. She hated him when he was like this. She hated herself. She felt as if she was suffocating. As the kettle begin to boil, her mind calmed and the knot in her stomach began to untwine. She wasn't going to let him take control of her. She wouldn't. She was going to apply for the receptionist job at the doctors. He couldn't stop her.

She went along for an interview a few weeks later after deciding she wouldn't need to even tell him about the job. It was only part time, two mornings a week so he need never know. She sailed through the interview and a week later was opening a letter asking if she could start work the following week. She rang Irene to tell her the news.

'That's great Maisie. It will do you good, get a bit of independence,' she told her friend. She worried about her, as an outsider she could see what a controlling hold Peter had over her.

'It's only two mornings a week, so we can still have our doggie walks the other days...and Irene...you won't mention the job to Pete will you?'

'Now how can I do that when the man hardly gives me the time of day! No don't worry Hun, I won't breathe a word. By the way, do you still need some help with the new flower bed? I can come round tomorrow if you are free?'

Maisie arranged that they would get together the next day to start on the new garden project. She wanted to create a new border along one edge of the garden. All country cottage type flowers interspersed with roses. But the ground was suffocating in ground elder so a major digging out was required. Irene said she would help and had another friend, Lesley, who could lend a hand too.

The next afternoon Maisie had already made a start. Her face was scarlet. She had been digging out a shrub that had looked half dead but was giving up a good fight to stay. Its roots went very deep and were entwined with ground elder. She knew it had to go but the heat of the day made it very hard work. She had stripped down to her shorts and a bikini top and began pushing her booted foot down onto the fork for another attempt when she heard voices from around the side of the house.

'You there Maisie?' Irene called as the side gate opened with Reggie bounding through with Irene close behind him. Maisie did a double take when she saw Irene's friend shut the gate behind him.

She jumped out of the deep trench she had excavated and grabbed at her tee shirt, slipping it hastily over her head.

Irene grinned, 'Maisie, this is my old school friend, Leslie.'

He put out his hand, 'Pleased to meet you,' his blue eyes smiled at her as he grabbed her muddy fingers and she felt the warmth of his hand against hers.

Maisie tried to regain her composure but her face continued to glow.

'Thank you so much for offering to help. I am finding it rather hard going. I've been trying to get this out of the ground for the past hour and still have tons of ground elder to dig up.'

'You look as if you could do with a drink Maisie. I'll go and get us something cold from your fridge, shall I?' Irene said, pleased at Maisie reaction to meeting Leslie.

She knew she was probably interfering but couldn't help it. She'd known Leslie for years, they'd always been like brother and sister but wasn't surprised at the mutual attraction. He was good on the eye and Maisie was a beautiful woman and both of them were kind souls. They were well suited she thought, much more than that domineering Peter.

When she returned with a tray of cold drinks and the cake she had brought along, she found Maisie and Leslie laughing together. Yes, she thought, maybe her plan would work.

Maisie's double life continued. She started the job and found it good for her self confidence. She enjoyed talking to patients, the doctors who worked at the little village surgery were friendly and the other office workers helped her learn the ropes and soon she was working the computer system with no problems.

The work in the garden continued. She tried to keep her eyes from Leslie's muscles as he dug through the soil. He was good looking and was also a really nice man. They shared so many interests and would spend hours discussing the merits of various authors whose work they enjoyed. Leslie also had a good knowledge of gardening and plants; roses in particular. He promised he would drop round a catalogue from a local nursery with some suggestions for plants that would look good in the new bed when it was ready for planting. At present, it looked like an archaeological dig with a six foot deep trench. The ground elder had really taken hold of the garden and they had dug very deeply to eradicate the pest.

Maisie's relationship with Peter began to alter. He was still the controlling man she had fallen in love with but the less time she spent with him the more she realised things had to change. She began to speak up for herself and one Saturday she had gone against his wishes and had a day out with Irene. He hadn't been pleased and didn't speak to her on the Sunday morning. She allowed herself to go back to being the meek and feeble Maisie for the rest of the day and he soon thawed out and took her to bed with a grin on his face. She still hadn't become pregnant, although the amount of times they slept together it was hardly surprising.

He rang her the following Thursday afternoon. She had been busy in the garden. Leslie had brought back bags of manure from the garden centre for her. They planned on digging it in the following week to prepare the soil for the planting. She heard the phone and left Leslie to it as she rushed inside.

'Maisie darling. I am so sorry but they want me to go to a trade fair this weekend. I won't be home I'm afraid,' Peter's apology sounded false.

'Really? Where are you going?' she asked. She knew he would be expecting her to say how sorry she was he wasn't going to be home. But she wasn't going to fall into that trap again. He was punishing her for going out with Irene. She knew that. But it wasn't going to work.

'Paris of all places. I would take you with me my sweet but there wouldn't be any free time. It's going to be work, work, work. I know you must be disappointed but maybe another time you can come too.'

'No probs Pete. You'd not want me there whilst you are working. I'll be fine. So, I'll see you Friday week?' she replied, pleased that her words were genuine. She really would be fine.

The next morning at work she began to feel a little remorseful. She hadn't done a thing out of line with Leslie but still allowed herself to feel guilty. She'd not told Peter about him and his help with the garden. She knew he wouldn't have approved. Leslie was such good company and although she loved Irene and looked upon her as her best friend she had to admit she looked forward to the days she wasn't free and she had Leslie all to herself.

She sat forward at her desk and checked through the post. There were the usual prescription requests and letters from consultants to deal with. She continued to open the envelopes and put everything in their respective piles. For filing, action or for the doctor. The last brown envelope was ripped open and out fell two small files. They were medical records requested from a new patient's old surgery. She turned them over. It was hers and Peter's records. It had been made clear at her interview how confidentially was paramount in her job so she knew she would be wrong to read them.

But they burnt a hole in her in tray as she dealt with morning surgery. She knew she could have easily just filed them away, out of sight but she left them, her fingers itching to look. Eventually the temptation was too much and as the last patient went into see the doctor she pulled the files out of the tray. She glanced around, the nurse on duty was on the phone and the manager was having a meeting with the other clerical staff and the head receptionist. She pulled out the papers from Peter's file and glanced down the notes. He rarely went to the doctor, or not since she had known him it seemed. There were lots of entries from before their relationship started and she began to decipher the notes about him.

She felt a cold rage sweep through her body as she continued to read. An accident. It had happened to him whilst he was still married to Angela. He'd been playing football with the boys. The notes had him as being signed off sick for some months. An injury, she read, a severe blow to the testicles. Internal bleeding. She put her hand to her mouth to stifle the cry. She looked around. The nurse had gone into her room. Behind the manager's glass door, she could see they were still in deep conversation. She continued to read.

The test results were there in black and white. Permanent damage to sperm production. Infertility.

She couldn't breathe. She wanted to shout. Scream. She had to keep this knowledge to herself. She shouldn't be looking at his records. The doctor's surgery door handle began to move and voices became audible. Maisie shoved the notes back into the file and hands shaking, threw it back into the tray, covering it with paperwork. She allowed her professional face to re-surface while she dealt with the patient, hoping he wouldn't notice her trembling hands and her heart pounding in her chest.

'Are okay Miss White?' Dr Howard asked, 'You are looking very flushed. I do hope you aren't coming down with a cold.'

She smiled and shook her head, 'No Doctor, I am fine thank you, really I am.'

That evening her head was full of questions. Questions she was unable to get answers to. Pete was away, but even if he was at home how could she ask him without admitting she had looked at something she shouldn't have? She began to argue with her self...but he hadn't told her something he should have. He had lied to her. He was infertile. Sterile. All his promises about talking about having children had been one big lie. No wonder he kept working away. No wonder he kept pushing to the future any idea of babies. The bastard!

She couldn't keep it bottled up. She would have to confront him about it. She tried his mobile but it went straight onto voice mail. She knew it would. He hardly ever kept in touch when he was away nowadays. Maybe he was doing to her what he had done to Angela? It had never crossed her mind until that moment that he could be unfaithful to her. She had always thought he loved her. But how could you love someone and lie to them as he had?

She had to talk to someone. She would burst with rage if she didn't. She would ring Irene and invite her round for supper. She would talk to her then. Hopefully sharing the problem would help.

She had remained in control when had she rang Irene to invite her round the following evening.

'Is everything okay Maisie?' Irene had asked, in her kind gentle voice, 'You don't sound yourself.'

Maisie's voice had quivered slightly. 'Yes, I'm good. Just tired. We can have a good chat tomorrow.'

As she replaced the handset her body finally released the anguish and pain and she wailed like a wounded animal. The tears flowed unabated and her body, jolted by huge wracking sobs, ached with the pain her heart was feeling. Finally spent of all her tears she went through the usual bedtime rituals. She checked the doors were locked, TV off standby and headed up to bed. She cleaned her teeth and wiped off her makeup. Swollen eyes stared back at her from the bathroom mirror. She took out the packet of contraceptive pills and the anger took hold. She screamed as she ripped the packet open and pulled it apart, the pills scattering over the bathroom floor. Throwing herself down she clawed at the tiny pills and began to sob once again.

'I hate you Peter! I HATE YOU!!' she wailed.

Saturday had arrived after a sleepless night. She felt sick and her chest ached from so much crying. She had forced herself out of bed and after standing under a steaming shower for twenty minutes she began to feel a little better. She indulged herself and sat with a bowl of cereal in front of the Saturday morning cookery and house hunting programmes. Anything to block out her thoughts.

It was late afternoon as she was beginning to prepare the food for supper that she heard a noise from the hallway. The jingle of keys. The door to the kitchen opened and Peter stood there smiling at her.

'Surprise! I managed to get out of the trip. Hey, you okay?'

She stood still, vegetable knife in hand and looked at him.

'Maisie, whatever's wrong?'

And still she stood staring at him. Silent.

'Maisie, you are frightening me now. What's the matter? Speak to me,' he began to walk towards her.

She held the knife forward, stabbing it in the air. The suppressed anger rising high within her.

'I know Peter! I know your secret!' she screamed at him.

He stepped back. Who was this woman? What had happened to his Maisie?

'Maisie, what is wrong? What have I supposed to have done? Tell me,' he pleaded.

'Don't lie to me!' she shouted, waving the knife at him, her face contorted with rage, 'I have been asking you for years about starting a family. 'Maybe soon Maisie" she mimicked, 'But NO! I know your secret...you bastard!'

'What secret?' his face flushed as realisation hit him. He stepped further back from the blade.

'Your accident. How fucking ironic is it...you didn't have the BALLS TO TELL ME!' She screamed at him and began to laugh. 'Permanent damage to your sperm production. I have read it Peter. I know! All this time you have led me on with promises...false promises!'

'I'm sorry Maisie...I am sorry,' his face crumpled. He began to cry, 'I wanted to tell you, I did,' the tears streamed down his face, 'But I thought you would leave me if you knew. I love you so much, surely you know that. I thought if you knew you would think me less of a man.'

She looked at him and saw the pain in his eyes. She saw the man he really was. Her anger melted away in an instant. She loved him. He had lied for her. She believed him. She understood now.

'Oh Pete, I am so sorry. How could I ever doubt you?' they both stepped forward. He held out his arms to her, his face wet with tears.

'Oh, Maisie I really am sorry. What can I do to make it up to you...Maisie!'

Her heart was booming in her ears, her mouth dry and she was shaking. She stood, knife in hand. Looking down she could see the blade and the red drops of blood slowly sliding down and onto the floor. They formed shapes on the kitchen tiles, spreading out like petals. For a moment, she had a strange thought that she was standing in a field of wild poppies.

How ironic, it was in a field of poppies where our love grew, she thought as her mind took her away from the horror of the moment and back to that day so long ago. A hot July day when she had run across the lane into the field with Pete running and laughing behind her. The sun had been warm on her shoulders and Pete had caught up with her and his hands on her arms had spun her round and kissed her, and told her they would be together forever and that he would never love anyone as much as he loved her.

She was unaware of doorbell as she sat on the kitchen floor stroking Peter's hair. It continued to ring in the recesses of her mind as she touched his still face with her hand, unable to comprehend what had happened. The knife lay on the floor, the blood now congealing. He had reached out to her. He had brought her towards him, pulled her close, hugged her tight. They had both forgotten about the knife, blade pointing outwards, that she still grasped securely in her hands in front of her chest. The blade had plunged deep into his stomach and his lifeblood pumped out from him as he fell from her arms.

'Maisie! Are you there? The front door was open,' Leslie pushed open the kitchen door and looked in at the scene.

'Maisie! What on earth have you done?'

Leslie had pulled her to her feet, taking her away from Peter. He tried to resuscitate him, bring him back to her but it was too late. Irene had arrived and between them they had forged a plan. Although they didn't know at the time that it had just been a terrible accident they stood by Maisie. She had watched, numb with shock, as they carried Peter's body to the garden and rolled him into the old frayed rug from the summerhouse. They carried their makeshift coffin up to the newly dug trench and gently lowered him deep within the soil.

Maisie was overcome with grief and despair and it was weeks before they managed to get the full story from her, by which time it was too late, it was a done deed. That day stayed with Maisie for the rest of her days, it was always there. Life went on around her but part of her stayed in that moment so she could still be with him.

Maisie looked in the mirror. He face was criss-crossed with wrinkles. Her milky grey eyes stared back at her in the mirror.

'Do I know you?' she said to reflection, 'You look familiar.'

She went into the kitchen and poured the boiling water into the teapot. Opening the cupboard, she reached in and took out her favourite cup and saucer. She had bought it to commemorate when young Prince George had married. That had been long ago now. A long time ago in her life. A life that had been wasted. It could have been so different. If only she had made different choices, where would she be now? She probably wouldn't have spent the past sixty years feeling full of guilt and fear. She looked out of the window to the garden at the wild red poppies growing in abundance on what would have been the carefully planned border. She knew now that you couldn't plan out your life, that you shouldn't plan it out.

    She'd made some wrong decisions. It will soon be time to see if she can put it right this time. She had to let her know. She had to keep trying until she listened. Tell her Maisie, tell her to think hard before she makes decisions, for she may not like the consequences.

    She let the young woman in and settled back into her chair beside her cup and saucer with the swirling gold pattern.

    'Do I know you?' she asked, 'You look familiar.'

The Bomber

Mum is calling me to come in but I want to see what happens. I see the last of the planes fly back over the channel and smell the fumes mixed with the salty air of the sea. I stand watching, pleased that they are going, but then I hear a rumble and I smell burning. A Nazi bomber! It's been hit He is floundering, not managing to keep control. A stream of smoke is billowing from the back. I watch as it gets lower and lower, nearing the woods to the edge of the village.

Looking back to the house I see that Mum has gone back inside so hopefully will not notice if I go and investigate. I run across the dry chalky soil and follow the retreating burning plane as it slowly loses all its power and descends with a scream into the trees.

I stop and watch as great clouds of smoke reach up into the blue summer's sky. Eagerly I run faster now towards the wood. I zig zag between the trees, along the paths. The smell of rotting wood mixed with the smell of burning metal and burning flesh fills the air. The plane, a smouldering gash in the canopy is still. No longer the evil killing machine it was when it left its homeland.

I take my time as I head towards the cockpit. What will I find? I step forward cautiously, stepping over the broken stumps, scattered twigs and branches around me. The window is smashed and I climb up and look. Blood has sprayed the glass, now polka dotted red. I gasp as I see the body of the pilot, head slumped forward, sticky blood oozing from his ear.

I hear a creak of metal and the plane moves slightly, sinking lower into its grave in the woods. I jump down and turn as I hear a rustle and then from the side of the plane he comes. One of the crew. He has survived. He stands, blood on his arm, he is holding it up against his chest with his other hand. He stares at me. I stare back. We are locked together. Who will move first?

Suddenly a commotion starts from the rooks from a nearby tree breaking the deadlock and so I turn and run and run. I run along the path towards the edge of the wood, ducking and diving in between trees and branches. I hear his footsteps getting further away as his injury must be slowing him down. I dart along a path to my right, taking a shortcut, hoping to outrun him. Turning to look behind, I don't notice the twisted stump ahead of me. I turn to continue on my way and trip and fall. The last thing I see is the huge stone on the ground that makes contact with my head.

I slowly open my eyes and look up to see the sky and clouds moving around above me like a spinning top. My head is throbbing and there is a searing pain in my leg. I feel my body juddering up and down and realise I am about three feet from the ground being carried by the crewman. His arm is bleeding badly, I can feel the wetness of the blood seeping out onto the back of my leg. Wriggling to free myself, he takes a firmer hold and looks down at me.

"halte stilles Kind," keep still child.

"Let me go you Nazi!" I struggle but it is no good, my head feels like a lead weight, I feel as if I am on a merry-go-round as the sky continues to spin and spin above me.

"To you home. I take you," he is stumbling slightly now and his grip has lessened from his injured arm. He looks down at me and smiles but I see in his eyes that he is in great pain.

I hear a seagull in the distance calling out 'kee-aar kee-aar,' then realise it's not a bird, it is my mother calling, "Peter! Peter!"

The German is staggering now but still carrying me across the grass towards my home. There are a few people just standing in the lane, watching. Mrs Beresford is holding on tightly to Wendy, who is crying. Mrs Roberts from number thirty is running towards the constable's house, shouting, "Come quickly. Help! It's Peter, it's Peter. He's been abducted by a German!"

I try to call out that he is helping me, that he is injured. Can't they see he is helping me? I try to tell them but my throat is so dry, my lips move but I cannot make a sound.

"Stille Stille." hush hush

My mother comes running over, "Oh Peter Peter! What have you done to my boy?"

The German moves his arms forward and nods to my mother to take me.

"You take your son, yes?"

I feel the warmth and comfort of my Mum's arms on my skin. I smell the faint smell of lavender from her neck as I lean up to her shoulder.

"He was helping me Mum, helping me," I say sleepily into her neck.

I jump as I hear gunfire and see the German has fallen to the floor, blood now covering his chest as Constable Black stands with his rifle aloft.

I sob, "But he was helping me."

The Bombers Tale

The boy is staring at me. He looks like a frightened rabbit. He cannot be any older that my young Axel. I don't know what to do. The plane is smouldering, a searing scorch mark in this wood.

England, it is a beautiful country. I came here during peace time and found it to be the green and pleasant land they say it is. I did not wish to go to war but I had no choice. What do I do? If I rebel against the Fuehrer's wishes it will not just be me that suffers but my beautiful wife and my young son. My best chance is to give myself up and hope and pray that I survive until the end of the war.

Suddenly there is a commotion. The crows are staging their own battle in the skies. The noise of the rookery brings the boy and myself back to the present. I can smell his fear, if only he understood me, I could tell him I mean no harm.

He runs from me. I decide to follow him, go to the people of this town and hand myself in. He is running fast, I am in pursuit. I do not want to lose him.

The ground below is very dry and stony, not easy to run fast after his young legs. The wound in my arm is beginning to throb as with each movement blood pulsates out from the gash.

I lose sight of the boy and walk cautiously along the path between the huge beech trees. As I pass them I see he has fallen. He is lying still on the ground, his leg twisted under him.

Ahead of me is a great expanse of grass and in the distance some dwellings. I put my arms around the boy. I touch his blond hair, so like my Axel. I see the people of the village out on the roadside, watching as I carry this young boy home to safety. They will be pleased that I have brought him back. Maybe they will let me write a letter to my wife to let her know I am safe before they take me to their prison camp.

The boy looks up at me. I smile at him and reassure him all is well. He is nearly home. I hope this terrible war ends quickly so I too, can soon be home.

I see the woman and she is crying. I pass the boy to her.

I see the barrel of the rifle. The war has ended for me.

Tudor Banquet.

Peter walked into the dining hall, satisfied with all that he saw. He loved the huge wooden tables; okay they were rather dented, scuffed and worn but it added to the authenticity. The walls were hung with tapestries that had been weaved with red, green and blue threads creating scenes from Tudor England.

His eyes surveyed the hall; pleased with the effect he had created. He glanced up to the gallery, his private domain high up in the oak rafters. It was where he housed his collection of busts. He had representations of all but one of Henry's wives. He was waiting for Anne Boleyn. The shoulder-stand, carved in white marble, sat empty in the glass case waiting for her. Peter had been looking for many years to find a face that he felt would do her justice. She had been a beauty beyond measure. He would continue his search. He knew it was only a matter of time before he would find the final piece for his display.

The fire within the Inglenook fireplace crackled and spat and the scent of the wood smoke filled the room. The sweet smell mixed with the aroma of the succulent pork that turned and glistened on the spit over the heat. The tables were set. Huge loaves of crusty bread and yellow, creamy slabs of butter punctuated the dishes of meats and fruits adorning the table ready for the banquet.

Peter had a love for everything Tudor. Well, maybe not everything, but he did love the bejewelled doublets, the women clothed in pearl encrusted velvet gowns, the merriment, the drinking, the eating, and the sex.

The Tudor period had captured his imagination when he had still been at school and Mr Harrison, the history teacher, had been droning on as usual. Peter's ears suddenly pricked up when he heard the words adultery, incest and fornication when Mr Harrison started to tell the tale of the trial of Anne Boleyn. Peter had listened avidly about the goings, and of course the comings, of Henry VIII.

Now after years of pouring over history books, watching films and generally absorbing everything Tudor, he owned and ran a company specialising in corporate events and organised Tudor banquets. He knew Henry would be proud of him.

The banqueting hall was almost ready and the waiting staff were making the final touches before the party arrived. Tonight, he was entertaining a group of Americans who were over from New York. They always got into the spirit of the event and tried to dress for the occasion. Peter watched as the first of the guests began to arrive.

'Oh, my God! This is just so like the films,' Esme stood in her purple velvet gown, mouth open as she looked around the room, 'Hey honey, come and see this,' she called to her husband, who was chatting to others of the party by the doorway.

Jerry, unhappily clad in green doublet and hose and a rather enormous and uncomfortable codpiece made his way into the hall, gazing up at the shield and sword adorned walls, amazed at all he saw.

'Gee! What a place. It's awesome!'

Peter walked over to greet the party before they were led to their seats.

'Good evening, welcome to Tudor Delights,' and he made eye contact with the waiting staff, who took his cue and escorted the throng of bodies into the hall and to their places.

Eyes grew large as they viewed the food piled high on the tables.

'I'm glad I went for elastic pants,' a guest twanged his waistband and laughed.

Peter stood by the door, smiling and indicating with his hand in the direction of the dining hall. People of differing shapes and sizes passed through the door in various costumes they deemed suitable to represent Tudor England.

Peter watched as the final few stragglers of the party walked up the steps and into the great entrance hallway. The two young women wore gowns of soft velvet and a young man was kitted out in a rather fine outfit with fur trim.

They hung back for a moment, having noticed a small wooden door slightly ajar, adjacent to the dining room entrance. Peter cursed to himself and rushed over to them. He would have to get the lock changed, that was the second time recently it had become unlatched. He didn't want people venturing up the stone staircase to his private area. The gallery was out of bounds to everyone.

As he strode across to them, he smiled and put his hand onto the door pushing it shut and secure.

'Sorry but this is a private area. Please do come inside and take your seats. The musicians are about to start and the feasting is about to begin,' he tried to chivvy them along.

The man in the fur edged doublet stood looking up the tapestries in the entrance hall.

'What a swell place you have here,' he ignored Peter's suggestions that they take a seat and dawdled by the door.

One of the women, wearing a rather tight fitting dress that emphasised huge mounds of flesh that undulated around her middle, reached up at one of the wall hangings, touching and pulling at the cloth.

'Hey Dean, feel this tapestry. It's so thick.'

Peter started to speak. He was about to suggest they were careful and could they please take their seats when the second young woman stepped forward.

'Dean, Betty, don't you think we should take our seats. We shouldn't really be messing with the decorations,' she looked across at Peter and smiled sweetly, 'I'm so sorry, we are holding up proceedings.'

Peter did a double take when he looked at her. She stood dignified and regal and looked at him with her dark almond shaped eyes. Her shoulders were bare and showed off her porcelain white skin and long elegant neck. Her dress was a soft blue and was enriched with pearls and sequins. Her full lips parted into a beautiful smile and she held out her hand.

'You must be Peter Edwards, I recognise you from your photo on the brochure. I apologise for my friends. We shall take our seats immediately,' She gave a little curtsey and dragged her friends across the great hall to the tables.

Peter watched as they walked across the dining hall and were seated. The beauty glanced his way and nodded and smiled to him and he gave a little wave. He had to put his lustful thoughts aside as he was dragged off by the head waiter to sort out a problem in the kitchen and from then on, he didn't have a moment to pause for breath while he conducted the evening like a symphony. Everything in tune and organised to perfection.

As usual the event was a great success and Peter watched as the guests sat in silence as the musicians played their final pieces.

As the soft voice of the singer filled the hall with her gentle rendition of Greensleeves, Peter made his way over to the tables. The beauty sensed his presence and turned her attention from the performance and looked at him and smiled.

Peter held out his hand to her and she slipped away from her friends without them noticing. They were sleepy from the heat of the fire and an evening of wine and good food.

Peter and the beauty walked out into the hallway. She'd had her fair share of drink during the evening and he'd made sure her last drink had been given an added ingredient.

'So, are you going to allow me to enter your private domain?' she tugged teasingly at his sleeve, 'I could see from the hall that you have many statues and busts up near the rafters.'

'Would you like to see the gallery at close quarters my dear?'

She leaned towards him and almost lost her balance as her vision started to become slightly fuzzy. He grabbed her forcefully by the shoulders to steady her and kissed her hard on the lips.

'Oh my, I am feeling rather woozy,' she grabbed hold of him and was aware that the tapestries were beginning to look out of focus.

As she slowly lost consciousness, he scooped her into his arms and opened the small door, carrying her limp body up the stone steps to the gallery where the glass cabinets that held his collection of busts had stood on display all evening. Their empty eyes stared vacantly at the revellers in the hall below.

All of Henry's wives were there. Apart from Anne Bolyen. But tonight, that would be rectified. He lay the beauty down on the marble slab and reached up and took down a sword from the wall. A sword from France for his beauty. Tonight, his collection would be complete.

The beauty began to regain consciousness, just time enough the see the sword whishing down through the air, down to sever through the porcelain white skin of her neck.

Voices in the Wood

Deep within the wood she waited. She had been waiting a long time. She eased herself up and walked across the dusty floor. Maybe it was time to go out and look again. She opened the great wooden door, brushed past the ivy and went out amongst the trees.

'Hurry up Val!' Kevin shook his head, wondering why she always seemed to make such hard work of everything she did.

He parked his bike by the side of the track and pushed his arms into his waterproof jacket. It looked as if the weather was on the turn. He'd heard rumbles of thunder and the sky was laden with rain. He stood and watched the slim figure of his wife as she struggled towards him on her bicycle. Her pretty face, framed with light brown curls, was grimacing with determination as she cycled along the rutted path. Kevin, tall, tanned and muscular, couldn't understand why she found cycling so difficult and he was feeling very impatient. He had hoped they would have been further along his planned route by now but Valerie had delayed them. She hadn't felt too well so they hadn't set off until after lunch for what he had hoped was going to be a pleasant cycle in the woods. Valerie was finding the route he had chosen very tough going but felt unable to put across her reservations. She was always hesitant to voice her opinions as he would often snap at her or put her down and slowly over the years she had lost her confidence.

Kevin got back onto his bike and continued to cycle on ahead along the bumpy woodland track. Valerie, slowly pressing each foot down onto the pedals with great effort followed behind, wondering why she agreed to a day cycling along the rough, rutted paths on the estate land.

There was another growl of thunder in the distance. The air was heavy with the imminent storm and the clouds were beginning to darken. A sudden flash of lightning lit up the clouds, silhouetting the trees against the skyline. The clammy air had brought out the mosquitoes in force causing Valerie more irritation as she continually brushed them away from her face.

She was feeling hot, tired and totally fed up. Fed up with the cycling and fed up with Kevin. She often fantasised about leaving him, but having no job or money of her own she didn't know what she could do. She felt trapped. He was so self- assured and confident. She knew it was unlikely he would ever understand how she felt, this feeling of suffocation.

Kevin stopped so Valerie could catch up and he took a swig from his water bottle as he sat half perched on his saddle looking across the grassland that edged the wood. The sky was angry and the trees were starting to dance in the increasing wind. If he had been on his own he knew he would be enjoying the day but turning and looking at Valerie's struggling figure moving slowly towards him made his heart sink.

God, she makes such hard work of it, 'Hurry up woman!'

Finally, Valerie's slow and laborious effort paid off and she was at Kevin's side. Her face red and sweaty, she retrieved her bottle from the holder and gulped down the water with eagerness.

'Blimey Kev, this is a very rough track, I don't think I shall be able to cycle much further, it's really taking it out of my legs.' She delved into the rucksack for her painkillers and had another swig of the water.

Kevin sighed and took out a map from the inside pocket of his waterproof jacket. Unfolding it, he placed it onto the saddle of his cycle. He was finding it hard to keep the map level as it thrashed about in the wind. He held the map down and indicated on the sheet with his finger.

'Look, this is where we are now. What we could do is take the fork to the left through this wood, see? Along through Devil's Copse, it's a bit overgrown, the path hasn't been maintained but it would cut off quite a few miles. Maybe you could cope with that? Want to try?'

She had hoped, as it was getting late and with the impending storm, that he would have suggested turning back to go home but realised she would have to grin and bear it otherwise she'd have his mood to deal with for the rest of the day.

'Yeah, ok, let's give it a go.' Getting back onto her bike she trundled along behind him into the wood.

The wind howled around them and suddenly the clouds burst forth a deluge of rain, within seconds they were both drenched. The shadows under the thick canopy of trees blocked out the charcoal grey sky. The trees creaked and moaned. Valerie glanced around, she didn't like it. She was scared, the wood felt sinister and threatening, as if she'd entered a forgotten world. The path was over-run with brambles and nettles and a great many of the trees were dead and decaying, standing like skeletons as they pointed their scrawny fingers towards her.

Kevin was managing to cycle along the muddy track quite easily but Valerie was finding it really difficult and was way behind and so missed being hit by the branch as it came crashing down. The almighty bough fell, striking Kevin and knocking him off his bicycle. Valerie let out a piercing scream and jumping down from her bike, lost her balance and fell awkwardly before coming to a halt on the wet ground.

She sat on the saturated earth feeling slightly dazed and peered through the fading light at Kevin's motionless body on the path. The rear wheel of his bike was twisted and bent like a modern art sculpture. He was on his side and the huge limb that had been ripped out of the tree by the great blast of wind lay across his left shoulder.

The earthy smell of damp decomposing wood and pine needles filled her nostrils as missiles of twigs and cones were thrown down onto the forest floor from the swaying canopy above. She knew it was only a matter of time before something else large and heavy would descend upon them again. She had to try to move Kevin and herself to a safer spot.

She pulled herself up, gasping as a sharp pain seared through her ankle. She ran her hands tentatively down her leg and felt around her ankle gently with her fingers. Hopefully it was just a sprain. Pulling out a scarf from her pocket, she bound it tightly around her ankle and satisfied that she had no other injury she eased herself up and moved carefully across to Kevin. A spark of guilt flashed in her mind as she recalled all the horrid thoughts she'd had about him earlier. Life with him was becoming more and more intolerable but seeing him injured and unconscious she felt a pang of remorse fill her sensitive soul.

She pushed at the hefty branch that had knocked him down, but didn't have the strength to move it. Brushing her rain sodden hair away from her face she leant over him and gave another shove. Kevin let out a moan. The branch was starting to give. She pushed with all her might and with a final thrust she was able to lever it off. Kevin yelled out in pain and lost consciousness again, his head falling back against a tree trunk.

'Kevin, don't worry, you're going to be ok, but we need to move away from this path,' she knelt down beside him, trying to ignore the pain in her ankle, 'Kevin, Kevin!' she rubbed his hand trying to wake him, 'Come on, see if you can move for me.'

It was no good, he wasn't going anywhere. The thunder was rumbling in the distance now, but the rain was still coming down in torrents. The wind blew the driving deluge into her face, pricking at her skin like sharp needles. She stood and looked around her. Dusk was falling, she needed to get help. But from where? She was surrounded by a maze of trees. As she was wondering which way to try she heard a faint sound from the bushes. She waited and held her breath and listened.

The wistful voice filtered through the wind, 'Where is Henry? Why will you not come to me?'

Was that someone in the woods calling for their dog? Whoever it was, maybe they could help her. She must find them fast.

'Hello. HELLO! Are you there?' she called out and listened again but the voice had stopped.

She headed off the main path and after a few minutes reached an opening in the canopy. She spotted a narrow track through a gap in the bushes at the other side of the clearing so she hobbled on in the fading light, feeling alone and small amongst the tall swaying trees. Losing all sense of time and direction she began to feel the terror of her situation. The noises of the forest echoed around her. She heard the eerie barking of deer in the distance and rustles from beneath the bushes. Petrified, she moved on quickly, walking faster now. The wet foliage brushed roughly at her face. Her waterproof jacket was saturated and her jeans were clinging to her skin. The headache of the morning started to throb again in her temples.

Panic rising, she stood amongst the trees not knowing which way to turn. She could see only thick woodland in every direction.

'Oh, my God, I can't...I can't do this! Where do I go, which way?'

It was then that a whimpering sound echoed through the forest. The rain had stopped and the muggy evening air was lifting the dampness from the ground in a swirling mist that rose up ahead like a steaming cauldron. Valerie knew her heart was beating too fast and her breathing too shallow. She tried to calm herself and get control. Maybe all she had heard was the dog that the woman had been calling to. She listened but all she could hear now was the raging wind in her ears.

The wind then hissed in her ears angrily, 'Where is Henry?'

Valerie shook her head, 'What was that? Who's there?'

The mist lapped up the floor of the forest, twisting like a snake across the bracken and ferns. The long thin skeletal fingers of the dark trees probed and poked at her. She spun around, trying to locate the source of the voice. Panic rising. Which way should she go?

'WHERE IS HENRY?' the wind shouted the words.

Fear soaring, she started to run, her injured ankle sending darts of pain up her leg. She pushed past bushes, running and running, faster and faster. The leaves and undergrowth flew past her as she raced along in fright. Then she stopped and looked ahead in absolute terror.

A dark and foreboding building towered high in front of her. The outside walls, edged with a carpet of nettles and weeds were punctuated with narrow leaded windows. Ivy wound its way up the outside and it twisted and curled itself around the rusty old bell that hung dormant in the tower that soared up through the trees.

Valerie took a deep breath and told herself that the wind and storm had spooked her. That was all it was. This building might be somewhere that could protect them overnight. Kevin was out cold and injured somewhere in the wood, but would she be able to find him again? She was lost, tired and all she wanted was to be home again. Tears started to flow. She couldn't believe how stupid she had been. She'd forgotten about the mobile phone! Why hadn't she thought to get the phone from Kev's bag and ring for help? How stupid she was.

Rooks suddenly dispersed from the nearby beech trees, cawing and shouting as they did so. Valerie moved tentatively through the long grass and weeds towards the grey stoned building. Her heart pounding in her chest, she walked cautiously around its perimeter and eventually came across an arched stone doorway. She looked up in the gloom and recoiled as she stared into the eyes of a grotesque creature carved into the crumbling stone, its tongue protruding from its mouth and a spindly finger pointing at her. All around the door were similar ugly faces and figures, all trying to deter visitors. Three worn stone steps led down to an old wooden door studded with enormous nails and a huge metal ring handle. She wondered if she dared enter. What was this place? Her question was quickly answered when she looked up to see a huge stone plaque on the wall announcing that it was the resting place for the McPherson family.

A mausoleum! There was no way she was going in there.

The soft whispers in the wind cried out, 'Henry! Henry!' Valerie stood on the stone steps paralysed with fear, 'When will you come to me? HENRY!' The voice was insistent and angry and louder now as the wind carried it around the wood.

Valerie's heart was pounding so hard, she thought she was going to faint. She drew on all her fading strength and courage and ran quickly down the steps to the door and slowly turned the handle. The door creaked open on its rusty hinges and she walked into the dark stone building, the home of the dead.

The silence hit her. The raging noise of the wind in her head was gone. It was dry inside and the storm was held back by the thick walls. Her eyes gradually became accustomed to the darkness. Shaking with fear she glanced around and in the shadows made out an alcove to her right where steps edged with large stone pillars rose high up into the belfry. In front of her was a narrow passageway leading deep into the shadows.

She was certain that if she ventured further into the building she would discover coffins and tombs. As long as she stayed where she was, by the entrance, she would be safe. She would stay away from where the coffins probably lay, up ahead in the blackness. But as her eyes took in her surroundings she froze. Out of the gloom she saw a sleeping figure of a woman. She looked so real, as if she would sit up at any moment and step down from the huge marble plinth on which she lay. Valerie could make out the folds of the dress and the delicate hands of the figure and right next to her was a large empty space. Valerie read the inscription beneath the woman's figure. It was a memorial to Francesca McPherson. The empty plinth beside her was inscribed for Henry McPherson.

Valerie leaned back against the door, shut her eyes momentarily and let out a long deep breath and tried to still her mind. She had to decide what to do. She didn't want to stay in this place. Should she try to find Kevin or should she go to find help? She must have been walking for over an hour to get to the mausoleum and was completely disorientated, with no clue as to which way she should go to get back to him.

Opening her eyes, she looked down at the dusty floor and her gaze hit upon footprints on the ground. She told herself not to panic; it's probably her own footprints she could see, but that was impossible! These were footprints of bare feet and they led from the side of the monument and headed towards the wooden door! Terror rose in her throat making it feel constricted, her breathing quickened, she started to feel dizzy.

There was a rumbling from the dark passageway and Valerie heard the sound of heavy stone scraping on stone. Then the voice started again, crying out, calling for Henry. At that same moment, the rusty old bell in the tower above her head began to awaken in the wind with an almighty toll. It clanged and crashed, loud enough to wake the dead. The ivy that had previously entwined the bell and held it silent came fluttering down. Then something heavier came plummeting down, bouncing onto the steps. A dead crow lay at her feet. The corpse began to move, its beak opened slightly and dozens of maggots squirmed and wriggled their way out of the putrid carcass. Valerie screamed, turned and ran blindly up the steps and away into the night.

Kevin awoke, pain searing through his shoulder. He was shivering. His waterproof jacket had been ripped open and he was soaked to the skin. He managed to sit himself up. Had he heard a scream or had it just been an owl? Where was Valerie? Slowly the earlier events replayed in his mind. His shoulder was throbbing and he suspected it was broken or dislocated but he couldn't stay where he was. Valerie was nowhere to be seen. He had to get help.

'Valerie,' his voice croaked out into the wind. Rummaging in his bag he found his water bottle and took a swig, 'Valerie! Valerie! Where the bloody hell are you?'

He pulled out his mobile phone and held it up with his good arm. No signal. Typical! He edged himself up and shuffled along, holding the phone high for signs of a link to civilisation. Nothing. He sank back down onto the forest floor as the trees above him rocked in the continuing gale.

Kevin dug into his rucksack for his fleece and pulled it around him as best he could, trying to ignore the pain in his left shoulder. He felt around inside his bag again and found Valerie's painkillers and took two, using the last of his water. Droplets of sweat were forming on his forehead but he was feeling so cold now. Every movement sent pain through his body but he knew he had to move, he had to get help.

Stumbling blindly along the path, he made his way towards an opening in the bushes where it looked as if the path was less overgrown. His legs felt like they would give way any moment but on he went, falling against trees and bushes as if intoxicated. The vegetation swayed around him, he couldn't focus properly. Hoping he wouldn't pass out he tried to get a signal again. He leant up against a tree and held the phone aloft. One bar! He started to key in 999 but the signal disappeared as quickly as it had arrived. He didn't know if he could cope much more with the pain in his shoulder. In desperation, gagging slightly as he had no water, he popped two more painkillers out of the packet and forced them down. As he stood by the tree he felt warm breath on the back of his neck.

He then heard a whisper by his ear, 'Henry.'

Not waiting or wanting to find out what it was, Kevin staggered away but then stopped dead in his tracks. Up ahead stood a woman. The evening mist was swirling around her long white gown and she was holding out her arms to him.

Kevin thought he must be hallucinating but then she spoke, 'You have come. I have been looking for you,' she began to walk towards him.

'Did Valerie send you? I really need to get some medical help,' Kevin muttered, before collapsing onto the ground.

Valerie sat by the fire clasping a mug of hot chocolate. She looked around the cosy room with a feeling of delight. Her feet were up on a stool and she could feel the warmth of the fire penetrating her body.

Gordon Plumrose came back into the room smiling, carrying a tray of sandwiches, 'Here we are my dear, you must be ravenous. What an ordeal for you, lost in the wood on a day like this. But do not worry, you are safe now,' he sat down next to her and patted her arm.

Valerie having run off from the mausoleum had travelled miles and eventually found herself on a dirt track. She had continued along the path for about half an hour, tired, wet and cold. When she had come across a small brick cottage she could have wept with joy. She staggered up the path and banged and banged at the door and it was eventually opened by a studious looking young man in a checked shirt, glasses propped on the top of his head.

Gordon had seen her bedraggled figure standing on his doorstep as he opened his door that evening. Before he could utter a word, she had fallen sobbing into his arms. Now here she was, sitting in the warmth of his home, being given so much care from this stranger. Care and comfort and kindness that was so alien to her. She had told him how she had been lost in the wood after hurting her ankle and somehow, she managed forget to tell him about Kevin. Gordon knew all about the Mausoleum and how people had reported hearing strange noises.

'Poor Francesca McPherson died young and it is believed she is calling for her husband Henry to join her in their joint tomb. She will have a long wait I'm afraid,' Gordon said as he passed Valerie another sandwich, 'Henry remarried only months after her death and when he died he was buried with his new wife elsewhere.'

Valerie looked at Gordon, munching on the sandwich, 'Poor Francesca, I suppose she is just lonely. She really spooked me though! I don't think I have ever been so scared.'

He took hold of her hand and held it gently, pleased he had finally met someone so lovely and sweet, 'Don't you worry. You are safe now.'

Kevin opened his eyes. It was pitch black. His left shoulder was still hurting and his hand felt weird too. The air was thick with decay. He tried to raise his head but there was something solid above him and he couldn't move. Where was he? What was going on?

He still had his mobile phone in his right hand. He slowly brought his hand up to his face and pressed a key. The screen lit up, the battery light flashing like crazy. He peered down. He could see his feet. He could feel his left hand being grasped tightly. He turned his head to the side and stared into the hollow sockets of the skull of the skeleton that lay beside him.

She kept hold of his hand, happy to finally have someone to share her tomb. She had been waiting a long time.

The battery warning bleeped. The light on the phone went out.

Silence in the Library

He switched off the kettle and listened into the silence. Yes, there it was again.

Tap tap tap.

He strained his ears trying to locate the source.

Tap tap tap.

David knew he was the only person left in the old building. He had been on the evening shift and the library had now closed. The staff from the offices below had long gone and the other library assistants had bounded down the staircase to freedom over an hour ago. He had stacked all the returns back on the shelves and was about to make himself a quick brew before setting off home for the night. The glow of the street lamp outside shone orange through the window giving a false sense of warmth. Once he had a hot drink inside him he would head out into the dark January evening. He was almost ready to leave, he'd checked the windows were shut and locked and had turned off all the main lights.

He walked over to the huge Georgian windows and looked down onto the high street. It was empty except for a couple of youths sitting on the wall by the bus stop. They were laughing, drinking from cans. The snow that had settled earlier that morning was now a slushy mess on the road but David could see against the light from the street lamp that large flakes were beginning to descend again. He'd best forget the tea and lock up and get home.

Tap tap tap.

He turned quickly and stared into the shadows. The sound seemed to be coming from one of the aisles in the modern fiction section. The air in the library began to feel heavy and momentarily he struggled to move.

'Who's there?' he called, as he walked back over to his desk and reached up to turn on the main lights but it stayed dark. David clicked the switch a few times with no success. The bulb in his desk lamp began to buzz and suddenly exploded in the fitting. David jumped back in alarm, his heart beginning to beat faster. He fumbled in the desk drawer and his hands finally located a torch. He began to walk along the end of each aisle of books pointing the beam down each row. It gave out a feeble light, flickered and then died.

Tap tap tap.

The shadowy shelves towered either side of him as he cautiously made his way down one of the dark narrow rows of books. As he reached the end of the aisle there was a sudden crash behind him. Startled, he turned and saw books tumbling down from the shelf onto the floor.

'Come on now, it's not funny. Come out.' he called out into the blackness, and he cautiously approached the avalanche of literature. He was aware of the sound of laughing from the boys outside and then the rumble of the engine of the bus as it set off to take them away. The streets would be empty now. No one around. The silence filled the library. The only sound, his heart thumping loudly in his chest. Time to get out of there. David quickly stepped over the fallen books and headed for the exit.

Tap tap tap.

The old radio on his desk gave out a low hum. It then started to hiss. White noise filled the library. The dial on the top began to spin around as if searching out stations. Voices and snippets of music echoed out in a jumbled mess from the speaker.

David made a dash for the door, 'Fuck this, I'm off.'

His fingers grasped at the door handle, twisting it round and round but the door would not give. He shoved his shoulder against the wooden panel, pushing with all his might, his chest tightening, heart racing.

Banging on the door he called out into the empty building, 'HELP. Is anyone still here? I'm locked in. Help me! Can someone help me!'

'I'll help you David,' a tinny voice spoke from the radio.

He froze. What the fuck was that? He turned from the door and his eyes locked onto the radio. He shouted a war cry like a mad man and ran towards the voice, snatched up the radio and threw it forcefully across the library. It shattered into pieces on the floor.

'What's up David? Feeling guilty about smashing in my skull?' the tinny voice called out to him from the mass of transistors and wires now scattered over the floor.

'I don't know who you are or what you are talking about. Just stop it and unlock the door.'

David peered into gloom. Maybe there was someone there messing with his head, playing a stupid, sick joke on him. The boys from the bus stop, maybe they'd sneaked in and were trying to scare him. He tried the light switch again but the library was still in darkness. He turned and twisted the door handle, shaking the door with all his might. It stayed shut. He had to get out of there.

'David, stay here with me,' the voice called out.

He remembered a T.V. show he'd seen about poltergeists. He'd seen what they could do. This building was old. Who knew what happened here in the past. Had something or someone come back to haunt the place? David shook the door handle, the door rattling in its frame but it wasn't going to give.

'Smashed my skull. Sitting waiting for my bus and you smashed my skull,' the harsh tinny voice shouted at him from the mound of radio parts strewn across the floor.

In a total state of panic David darted across to the old sash window and tried to yank it open. The lock was jammed. He then noticed the heavy old paperweight on top of a cabinet, picked it up and banged it against the lock. He tried again to open the window. It wouldn't quite budge. He slammed the paperweight hard against the lock again, bashing it with force and this time it not only managed to break the lock but also the pane of glass and the paperweight left his hand and went crashing down from the first-floor window to the street.

He heard a scream. A scream from the bus stop below. He looked down to see a woman lying still on the ground. The blood from her skull was trickling out onto the fresh layer of snow.

'See - smashed my skull, didn't you?' hissed the radio.

The Legacy

Philip made his way down the stone steps and was confronted by a wall of boxes. He decided today was the day he was going to tackle the final unpacking. Julia was clattering about upstairs in the kitchen, still trying to find a home for the pots and pans.

They had recently moved to a little Norfolk village when Philip had taken a post of G.P. in a nearby town. He'd started work almost immediately so hadn't had a great deal of time to sort through all the boxes he had put down in the cellar when they had first moved into their new home.

He'd fallen in love with the cottage at first sight with its courtyard garden overlooking the ruined castle. The dark living room had steep wooden stairs leading up to a narrow passage with no windows. It did make it gloomy but Philip loved the fact that when he opened the bedroom doors it was like walking into another world. Out of the darkness into a room full of light. The rooms seemed to call him in. He would sit by the window, looking across to the stone walls of the ancient ruins, watching the birds gathering twigs and moss to build their nests. No problems for them with lack of cupboards, lack of space. He was envious of them, waking each morning singing their joyful song.

Although it was smaller than their previous home Philip felt the place had soul. Julia however wasn't convinced and was finding it hard living there. She had told him she felt that something was watching her when she walked up the stairs and a few nights ago she had woken him, hissing in his ear.

'Philip – can you hear that? Listen…screeching.'

He slowly opened his eyes, 'What's the matter? I can't hear anything.'

'It's stopped now, but I did hear a horrid screeching noise.'

'Probably an owl, go back to sleep, stop spooking yourself.' He turned over in bed and for brief moment thought he saw a faint figure standing in the doorway but assumed it was just shadows in the darkness.

He sighed as he sat down in the musty cellar, picked up his knife and started to open a cardboard box stuffed full to the brim with books. Sitting on top of the old medical textbooks was a paperback about the village and its history.

He frowned. How strange, he didn't recall owning the book, he'd never seen it before. He picked it up and flicked through a few pages. It did look interesting so he promised himself he would find time to read it and maybe learn more about his new village.

There was more clattering from the kitchen and banging of cupboard doors and he felt his shoulders tighten, as he knew what would come next. He heard curses then footsteps running down the cellar steps.

'Philip, Philip, I really can't do this. There's no room for anything!' she slumped down on the packing case next to him, holding her hands to her face, letting out a sigh.

He leant over and took her hand, 'I know it was difficult for you moving away, but please be patient. I'm sure you'll grow to love it.'

She looked up at him, 'I'm sorry Phil but I really do wonder if I will. I feel so lonely and isolated and it wouldn't be so bad if I loved this place, but I don't. I feel uneasy. It feels as if there is someone in the shadows staring at me and it's cramped, smells damp and I miss my friends,' she started to sob.

He stood up and pulled her to her feet, 'Why don't you ring Carol and see if the two of you can have a few days away together?' he said, trying to be sympathetic, 'Go on, give her a call.'

He sat back down on the steps and tried to hold back his anger. He had been feeling so wound up these past few weeks. Starting his new job was stressful enough without having Julia moaning all the time. It wasn't long before the sound of her laughter filtered down to him. Her silly giggle grated on his nerves and the fury slowly rose in his chest as the constant suspicions filled his mind. Was it really Carol she was talking to? He shook his head and tried to push his doubts away but the tightness in his jaw lingered as he ripped across the top of another box with his knife.

Lying in the bath later that evening he felt more peaceful. It felt good to wash the grime of the day away. The old local history book lay beside him, he planned to read it in the bath but for now he was savouring the sounds and smells of the evening. The small window was ajar and he could hear the gentle hum as the bees gorged on the sweet-smelling honeysuckle flowers outside.

It reminded him of his childhood and visits to his grandparents' old cottage in Suffolk. His grandfather, John Eagle used to thrill him with tales of witches and bogeymen and he would sit enthralled and slightly scared.

Grandfather would peer over his glasses, 'Not frightening you too much am I boy?'

'No Gramps! Tell me again about the old witch in our family again– what happened to her?'

'Well boy, the story goes that she was married to Ethan Eagle, who was a very strict man with a fiery temper and she did something real bad,' he moved nearer to Philip, enjoying watching his eyes widen. Philip knew what was coming next, he'd heard the tale so many times but loved hearing it again, 'So bad, that,' Gramps paused for effect and leant even closer, 'So bad that he killed her and bricked her up in the walls of the house!!'

Philip smiled as he remembered the happy times with his grandfather. He knew his family had originated from this part of Norfolk and he'd been meaning to trace back and find out more but never seemed to have the time. He picked up the history book and looked inside, still bemused as to its origins. It wasn't his book that was for sure. He flipped through the first few pages to see if there was a clue. Apart from the publisher's details all he could see was the words 'You will pay' written in a spidery hand. He had no idea what it meant, maybe it originally referred to the price. He lay back in the bath and began to read snippets about the village. It used to be a stopping off point for pilgrims heading up to Walsingham. The pilgrims used to visit the priory in the village too, to look upon the relic of the arm of St Philip.

He thought maybe he would take a stroll there soon and see if his namesake's arm was still there, and if the good weather continued he could sit and have a drink in the pub, have another chat with Rob, the landlord, who was also fairly new to the village. It was a quaint old pub and they served a good choice of food. Philip had taken Julia for a meal there a few weeks ago, hoping a night out together would be a little light relief from all the moving in chores and maybe they could have a conversation that didn't end up with an argument.

They had been eating their main course when Julia suddenly announced, 'I think I may make up the bed in the spare room. I've not slept at all well since we moved here, maybe if I'm on my own I will.'

Philip had felt the burning anger start to rise. She had made no effort at all to make a go of it. After her announcement, they had sat in silence while they continued their meal. The minutes ticked by and he felt a tightness in his chest as his tension grew. His mind went into an endless loop of jealous thoughts, imagining Julia sleeping with another man. How he despised her for it. It was difficult to hold his feelings in check as he sat opposite her, knowing she no longer wanted him. Unable to contain his anger, he jumped up, his chair scraping harshly on the slate floor and he went to the bar to order another drink. Landlord Rob, who was drying glasses, caught his eye and walked over and pulled him a pint.

'Everything ok? The food alright?'

'Yeah, no problems thanks, except for the wife!' he laughed and took a swig of his beer.

'You settling in okay to the village? Nice little place, isn't it? Nice and peaceful – although it does have its dark side so I have heard.'

Intrigued Philip sat down on the bar stool to hear more. He would leave the old hag to sit and eat her meal alone, if that is what she wanted.

'So, what is the dark side about the place then?'

Rob leant across the bar, 'Well, I was talking to one of the regulars, and as I am new to the area too, he thought he should fill me in with some local tales. Loads of them, all a long time ago mind you! There's the gravedigger who tried to make some money by selling the corpses for medical research, and then there's the wife murdered and bricked up in the walls of the house, and also the tale of the lepers who used to walk along outside the priory…'

'Hold on, hold on, what's this about a woman bricked up? Where was that then?' Philip finished his beer and put the glass down ready for a refill.

'Yeah, that was a good tale that was. Not sure why he murdered her, or if she's still bricked up. But I was told that the hubby got away scot free, had friends in high places it seems.'

'Do you know his name? Wasn't Eagle by any chance?'

'Sorry mate, no idea,' Rob answered before going to serve some new customers who'd just arrived.

As the cold bath water brought Philip back to the present, a faint breeze wafted in through the window raising goose bumps onto his damp flesh. Lost in his thoughts he had forgotten he still had the book in his hand. He quickly moved to get out of the bath but dropped the book into the water.

'Bugger! Oh no, it's soaked!' he pulled the dripping pages out of the bath and quickly wrapped it into a towel to try to absorb the excess water before taking it along the hallway to the airing cupboard, hoping that it would dry out.

As he sat naked on the bed, rubbing himself dry he heard a scratching sound coming from the bathroom so he trotted back along the passageway to investigate. He stopped in his tracks in the doorway. The air in the bathroom felt icy cold and wispy tendrils of freezing mists floated around the room. A stiff breeze was blowing in through the window, dislodging the honeysuckle that now tapped rhythmically on the glass. But Philip disregarded this for his eyes were focused straight ahead at the mirror on which was scrawled in the steam the words, 'you will pay.'

He slowly approached the mirror as the steam faded and he found that all he could see was his own face looking back at him. Shivering slightly, he leant over and shut the window and quickly left the bathroom and went back to the bedroom to get dressed.

It was a few days later and Philip, having the place to himself, had taken a few days off work to sort out the mess in the cellar. The day promised to be a scorcher, so leaving the chores until later, he decided to take a stroll to the priory ruins. He made his way up the narrow street lined with flint stone cottages towards the towered gateway that led to the village green. It felt peaceful. Swallows were swooping down between the buildings, sparrows were chirping in the eaves and a blackbird was singing its beautiful liquid song. It was good to have some time alone without worrying about what to do about Julia and his heart was singing with joy like the birds.

He walked slowly up the road and under the Bailey Gate, savouring the peace. He was surprised how quiet it was, usually it was busy with people visiting the village, but today there wasn't a soul around. As he walked past the empty al fresco seating of the tearoom, its sign swayed and creaked in the gentle breeze. He skirted around the exterior wall of the churchyard and headed down the lane to the priory. He glanced around, bemused that it was so devoid of people; there was no one to be seen. The earlier sound of birdsong was gone. He had never seen it this quiet and hushed.

Philip continued along the road in the direction of the priory ruins, the loose stones on the road crunched beneath his feet. The sky was cloudless and the blazing sun was scorching everything in its wake. He turned into the lane to his left, and made his way down the hill towards the river, hoping that the cool water's edge would be more refreshing in the heat. He could see the priory ruins across the fields and noticed movement in the distance. He could just make out the figure of a woman in a long dress heading across the path towards him and the river. The sun was so bright it made him squint and when he looked again all he could see were the ruined walls, stark against the sun -bleached grass.

He stood leaning on the bridge over of the ford, looking down into the clear sparkling water and thought again of Julia's constant whinging. She had told him that she felt stifled by village life and had moved with him under sufferance. She preferred life in the city and hadn't been best pleased when he had announced he'd applied for his job. But Philip believed she had other reasons. He'd suspected for some time before the move that she had been seeing someone, having an affair. There had been furtive phone calls and the sudden renewed interest in her appearance.

He recalled how unresponsive she had been when he told her his application had been successful. She had ignored him and picked up a magazine and started reading.

'Julia, did you hear me? I've got the post in Norfolk! Surely you must have something to say?'

She looked at him over the top of the magazine, gave him an icy stare, then flung down the magazine and flounced off to the bathroom. He heard the gush of the shower and knew she was obviously planning another night out with her friend.

Naively, he had thought moving away would be a new start for them, maybe bring them closer together, but it wasn't to be. He felt hurt that she didn't support him in his new job and he had found that his anger and bitterness had started to grow even more when they moved into the cottage.

Suddenly a jet from the nearby airbase thundered across the sky, breaking Philip's contemplation. Deciding it was too hot to cross the fields to the priory, he started to make his way back up the steep hill towards the village, and took the short cut through the churchyard. The heat of the day slowed down his steps and he took time walking past the gravestones. He heard no footsteps so was surprised when a tall woman wearing a long green dress strode briskly past him towards the churchyard gate. Her hair glistened like polished copper in the sunlight as it hung down in a long plait down her back. She went through the gate and then disappeared from view.

Philip continued to walk slowly amongst the graves, many old and crumbling, the lichen devouring the inscriptions. He started to read the wording on some of the old stones and his eyes fell on a couple of graves near the path inscribed with his surname. Excited with his discovery and that they may be his kin, he started to walk on the grass amongst the older stones, many sinking into the ground almost out of view. He then spotted a headstone right near the edge of the graveyard. Although it was very old it looked well-tended and there was a fresh bunch of wild flowers lying on the grave. He peered closer. He was sure the surname on the stone was Eagle but couldn't make out much more of the inscription. He knelt on the grass in front of the stone, the smell of the honeysuckle floated up and filled his nostrils with its sweet scent. He pushed the flowers to one side and began to rub at the stone to try to make out the wording but the grave wasn't keen to give away its secrets.

A voice from behind him said, 'Not very easy to read, is it?'

Philip turned to see a short grey haired man in a dog collar.

'Save your fingers young man, I can tell you about that stone if you wish.'

Philip scrambled to his feet, 'Just thought it interesting, being so old but obviously well-tended. Who was it?'

'Poor woman, I do wonder if she will ever be at peace,' said the pious looking man of god, 'I like to let her know the Lord is thinking of her, so I lay the flowers on her grave. Although whether she is down there in God's good earth is questionable.'

Philip walked slowly with the vicar towards a bench in the churchyard, 'Why do you say that? Why wouldn't she be? Who was she?'

They both sat down in the shade and the Rev Johnson smiled, 'Her name was Matilda Eagle and poor woman was branded a witch in her day. Helped people who were sick, supplied them with herbs for their ills. Story goes she helped one man a bit too much, if you get my drift!' he chuckled to himself.

Philip turned to the vicar, 'So why do you wonder if she is actually in the grave? Where else could she be?'

'Well, she could be there, there again she might still be bricked up where her husband put her after he murdered her, we may never know. The vicar before me had to perform a blessing down near the castle as strange things kept happening, people kept hearing things that seemed not of this world, screeching sounds they said, terrible, terrible noises. If it is to do with her, well, I just hope she finally gets some peace.'

Philip couldn't believe what he was hearing. It matched the story from all those years ago told by his grandfather, this must be the woman. He never really thought it was actually true but maybe it was!

Philip was about to ask some more questions when a young couple came through the gate and approached them, 'Sorry to interrupt Rev Johnson but we are waiting to see you to discuss our wedding, you said to come along at midday?'

Rev Johnson got up and turned towards Philip, 'Sorry to cut short our little chat, don't mind me. Take what I say with a pinch of salt, probably nonsense!' And off he went.

Philip sat alone on the bench trying to take in all he had been told. The vicar had said a blessing had been done near the castle and that must have been near his cottage! Crikey! Julia had said she thought she heard screeching. Maybe it had been the adulterous witch after all. He needed to get more details. Maybe Rob at the pub might be able to tell him more. He went over to the grave again and stood looking down at the stone. He felt his muscles tense. So, this may be the jezebel that his grandfather had told him about, the one who cheated on Ethan Eagle. A sudden fury rose from the pit of his stomach.

'Cheating Whore!' he sneered and kicked at the delicate flowers on the grave, scattering them across the grass. Words echoed in his head as if spoken by an outside force.

'Bitch!'

'So, you went with another man then, did you?'

'Whore!'

His rage subsided and he started to make his way to the road, heading for the pub. Inside the bar was packed with people, no way he'd get to talk to Rob today, so he wandered out into the garden with his drink. All the tables were occupied. It was a contrast to earlier, noisy now, and full of life.

He stood with his beer, leaning against the wall of the pub, sheltering from the sun in the shadows and his thoughts dwelled on the grave of the Eagle whore. Feeling his temper re-surfacing, he forced his mind elsewhere and thought about the woman who had dashed past him in her long green dress. She had a familiarity about her even though he was sure he hadn't seen her in the village before. She was too striking to be forgotten, but there was something about her that resonated within him. Finishing his beer, he made his way back outside and started to head home.

As he approached the Bailey Gate he was aware again of the sudden calm, as if time had stood still. It was so different to the earlier noise and hubbub of the pub. He stood straining his ears for a sound of life, but even the birds were silent. As he walked down the road towards his cottage, he caught sight of the green dress as the woman turned into the footpath that passed by his cottage.

It was as he was opening the front door that he heard a noise in the garden. A shadow moved across the side fence just before the sun disappeared behind a cloud. He stepped back from the door and peered around the corner.

The woman in green was standing in his garden with her back to him. As he approached her she twisted around to face him. His heart missed a beat. She held her hands to her stomach. It was covered in thick dark blood, seeping through her fingers and soaking the front of her dress, slowly spreading out on the material, forming shapes. She was quite motionless, her eyes dark and piercing, looking at him. Her skin was deathly white and as she stood, he felt her stare penetrating his very soul.

It was then that she tilted her head heavenward and let out a long piercing screech. On and on she screeched. He held his hands over his ears as the screeching stabbed at his eardrums. The wind suddenly picked up, and lashed at him and he was blown against the wall of the cottage and all the time she stood, shrieking into the air. And when he felt his ears could take no more, she suddenly faded and was gone and all was still.

Philip turned and rushed inside, feeling dizzy, heart racing. He bolted the door behind him and stood for a moment with his back against the door, trying to calm himself. He tried to make out in his mind what had happened. Who or what had he seen? Was it the ghost of Matilda Eagle?

He moved cautiously over to the window and glanced out. Everything looked normal, no one about. He took a glass from the cupboard and ran the tap, gulping down the water, trying to cleanse himself of the evil that seemed to be filling his soul.

It was as he was putting the glass again to his lips that he heard a clattering from the cellar. Bracing himself to go and investigate, he went to put the glass on the worktop, and it was then that the screeching began again. The glass smashed in his hand, splinters of glass cascaded around his fingers, cutting into his flesh. He held his bloodstained hands over his ears, and begged the noise to stop. After a few moments, all was quiet again.

He knew he had no option but to go down into the cellar.

Going tentatively down the stone steps, he put his hand up to the light switch. It didn't work. There was a sudden gush of air and the cellar door slammed shut behind him. He stood on the step of the cellar in the blackness. Suddenly the screeching started again, hitting the walls, ricocheting back and forth. So loud, on and on. Penetrating every corner. He stood rooted to the spot, hands over ears, eyes tightly shut, praying that the moment would end.

Suddenly all was quiet, all was still. He cautiously tried the light switch again and the fluorescent tube flickered into life. There, standing just a few feet in front of him, was Matilda. Staring at him. The blood on the front of her dress forming the words 'YOU WILL PAY.' The light flickered on and off for a few seconds and then she was gone. The white walls of the cellar reflected back in the bright light as Philip's eyes darted around the musty space. Everything was as he had left it except for the local history book. It was now lying open at the bottom of the steps.

Heart still crashing in his chest, he sat on the step and picked it up. It was open at a page about this very cottage. He read the tale that many generations ago Ethan Eagle had lived in the cottage with his wife, until he murdered her because of her adultery. Her body never found, some say it was bricked up in the cottage. It's said she vowed before she died that if her husband didn't pay for his crime, one day one of his kin would pay.

He looked across the cellar, the stark white light shining on Julia's bloody corpse where he had left it some days before, her eyes staring blankly at him in death.

He then thought he heard the piercing scream again but realised it was a police siren.

Rev Johnson was in the pulpit when he heard the police sirens and he smiled. Continuing with his sermon he spoke, 'The reading today is from Exodus 34. He will by no means leave the guilty unpunished, visiting the crime of fathers on the children and on the grandchildren to the third and fourth generations.'

Later, out in the graveyard, Rev Johnson walked over to Matilda's grave and gathered up the scattered flowers and gently put them back neatly in place. He stood for a moment and listened. All was still, all was quiet, all at peace. He smiled. His work was done.

Isobel

The sun was high in the sky as Isobel opened the gate to the recreation ground. She hitched up her bag, the weight of the school books pressed into her shoulder. The clear blue sky promised her an afternoon in the garden whilst revising for tomorrow's last exam. She was glad they were nearly over. Glad she could see the holidays ahead.

She'd decided to head off home after today's maths paper, the others had stayed behind in the library to study. Isobel knew not much revising would be done, just giggling and reading of magazines. She was glad to get away from them. They were alright as friends but they didn't see the importance of exams. They thought clothes and makeup were the most important things in the world. If she'd been in the higher- class things might have been different but her course work dictated that she was not worthy of being in the A stream even though she really enjoyed learning.

She wandered over to the edge of the river. It flowed through the park and then headed down past the church and into the field beyond. The water level was quite low today. There had been no rain for weeks, the grass was parched. She was parched. She delved into her bag for a bottle of water and was nearly knocked over by a little dog that darted past her and scampered down to the river. Within moments the air was filled with the sound of barking as he struggled to get back up the sandy riverbank.

Isobel slung her bag down onto the ground and knelt on the grass, leaning over to look at the dog. However much he tried, and try he did, he couldn't make it back up the bank. Isobel slid head first down the incline, arms outstretched to reach him.

She was tall. Lanky Little, they called her at school. She would laugh with them but inside it hurt. If only she wasn't so tall, if only her surname wasn't Little. Her first name didn't help either.

'Is a bell little?' they would say, 'Well if it is, it won't make much noise will it!' they laughed. Isobel would smile and try to stop her eyes smarting as the tears threatened to appear and she'd get the tell-tale sting at the back of her nose.

But being lanky was in her favour today. She managed to get almost close enough to touch the little dog but not quite. He had stopped barking and was sitting with his back legs immersed in the water, holding his head to one side, as he looked up at her above him. She held out her arms and tried to encourage him to her.

'Come on fella, come on, I'll help you out.'

'Don't think he wants to go with you.' a voice said from behind her. A male voice.

She was startled and began to slide down on the loose soil, just managing to stop herself journeying headlong into the river. As she let out a slight cry of alarm, the dog rushed past her, up the bank and bounded off as fast as his short little legs would carry him.

The male voice behind her began to laugh.

Now feeling annoyed, she managed to slide herself backwards up the river bank, hoping her skirt wasn't riding up too high as she did so. Feeling hot and flustered she turned red faced and sat on the grass, rubbed at the soil that was now embedded in her palms and looked up to see who was mocking her.

It was Peter Richardson! Oh, my goodness! She had worshipped him from afar for three years now. Every morning on her way to school, he would walk past her in the opposite direction as he headed off to the grammar school. She knew his name, knew lots about him. She'd fished for information from friends of friends. His sister, Veronica, went to the youth club and Isobel had tried to befriend her, hoped she could get to him through her but Veronica didn't want to know Isobel, a lowly secondary school girl. But now here he was, standing over her, just as she had made a complete fool of herself and he was laughing at her.

She jumped up, straightened her skirt and watched as the speck of a dog disappeared into the distance towards the church. Her cheeks red with heat and embarrassment, she bent down to pick up her bag and sneaked a look through her lowered lashes at Peter. He had stopped laughing now and was standing watching her, smiling.

'There's not many who'd have gone to so much trouble to help a little dog. What a pity he didn't appreciate it,' he said as he picked up her water bottle, wedged beside a stone where it has fallen when the dog had jumped up and ran off. He held it out to her. She felt a tingle as their fingers slightly touched.

'I am sorry I laughed. I wasn't laughing at you, you know. It was just so comical seeing the dog run off like that. I think he belongs to the old guy who lives in the end house by the church.' he indicated towards a row of old stone cottages at the far end of the park. 'I've seen the dog from a distance most days. It sits and looks out through the front gate.'

Isobel had been using the time that Peter was speaking to calm herself and try to stop her heart from beating so fast. It was the closest she had ever been to him, usually it was just a furtive glimpse as they both dashed past each other on route to their respective schools. Now she could see that his eyes were a deep brown, his lashes too. His dark hair rested on the collar of his white school shirt.

She found her voice, 'Do you think we, sorry that is, I. Should I go and see that the dog has got home okay? The road over by the church gets busy later when the mums pick up the little ones from the playgroup.'

'Good idea. I'll come with you, Isobel. That's if you don't mind?'

She shook her head, 'No, that's fine with me.' He knew her name! How did he know her name?

They walked slowly across the sun-bleached grass. He began to tell her about his exams. He too only had one more to go.

'I'll be glad when they are over, although it'll probably be worse then, as we have to wait for the results. How do you think you've done?'

She shrugged, 'Not sure. I hope I've done okay. I'd like to stay on for sixth form if I can. But it's probably not that likely.'

She tugged at her bag as it fought with her shoulder. The heavy books dug a ridge into her skin.

'You may surprise yourself,' he smiled, as they neared the row of old cottages. 'No sign of the runaway dog in the garden. Maybe we should knock and see that it's got home okay, and if not offer to look for it.' He hesitated, 'That's if you have time that is?'

'Yes, yes I have. I was only heading home for more revising,' she pulled a face at the thought and then wished she hadn't. He probably thought she was ugly now.

He didn't. He thought she was beautiful. He'd watched her dash past him most mornings on the way to school and hoped one day he'd pluck up courage to talk to her. He'd found out a bit about her but he didn't think she'd be interested in him. She was gorgeous, tall and slim with long legs. Her blonde hair, cut in a long bob bounced about when she moved her head.

He forced himself to stop thinking about her legs, 'I've seen the old chap who lives here. He'd probably welcome our help. I doubt if he could venture far to search for the dog, he's really bent double.'

They shut the gate behind them and walked up the path. The house was quiet as they rang the bell. No dog barking at the visitors.

'Doesn't sound as if anyone is in,' Isobel said after a few minutes of waiting at the doorstep.

They went to turn and leave when they heard a rattle and a clunk and slowly the door opened. A wizened old face with milky eyes appeared. A few wisps of wiry hair on a balding head, hunched low in front of bent shoulders giving him the appearance of a vulture.

'What do you want? Do I know you?' his voice croaked at them.

'Sorry Sir,' Peter began, 'But we wanted to check your dog got home okay. He was loose over the park and then ran back in this direction.'

'We were worried about him being out on the road,' Isobel added.

'Dog? Dog? I haven't got a dog,' he shook his head, looking confused.

'I am sorry, my mistake. I thought the little brown and white dog was yours. I often see him in your garden.'

The old man's eyes filled with tears. He pulled out a huge grey handkerchief from his trouser pocket and wiped at his eyes, shaking his head, 'Roddy. It must be Roddy. You've seen him you say?'

Isobel put her hand on his arm, 'Please don't be upset. It's the last thing we wanted to do, upset you. So, is Roddy a neighbour's dog?'

Although he was obviously moved by something they had said, his eyes began to take on a brightness and he smiled a toothless grin as he leaned heavily on his walking stick, 'I can't stand here much longer. You best come in. If you want to hear about Roddy that is?' He indicated with his bent head to the hallway beyond.

Isobel looked at Peter. Her eyes questioning if he felt it safe to go inside. He nodded and held her arm as they followed the hunched old gentleman into his sitting room. A blue budgerigar was flying about the room, startling them both momentarily. It finally landed on the back of one of the armchairs. It started to peck and pull at the threads of an old tablecloth that was draped over the back of the chair for protection. Not that the chair needed much protection, the cushion was giving up its filling in lots of places.

Peter put out his hand to the bird and it hopped onto his finger. 'I love budgies. We've a green one at home, her name's Dinky, but she's not as tame as this chap. He's a beauty.'

'Yes lad, that's Joey. Just the two of us now. We used to have loads of animals about the place, but just me and Joey now.'

'Well, he must be good company for you, Mr...?'

'My name's Harry lad. And this,' his bony fingers picked up a photograph and he held it up in his shaky hand for them both to see, 'This is me on my wedding day with my lovely Phyllis.'

They both peered at the picture. Harry looked very dapper in a double-breasted suit and Phyllis was smiling at the camera in a long white bridal dress. And at their feet, a little brown and white dog.

'Oh, my goodness, the dog! It looks like the one we saw in the park,' Isobel exclaimed.

Harry carefully placed the frame back on the sideboard and lowered himself into the chair. The budgerigar flew onto his shoulder and began to nibble at his earlobe.

'Yes, that little dog was our Roddy. It was because of him that Phyllis and I met. He knocked her over, scampering about in the park he was. I came along and helped her up. Love at first sight.' He shook his head and smiled, 'Police said he was a stray, so he came and lived with us. We had many a good year together. Broke our hearts when he finally died.'

'What happened to him Harry?' Isobel asked.

'He was such a rascal right to the end, bit too adventurous for his own good. He fell in the river, got caught up in the weeds. A young woman saw him, brought his body back to us.' He wiped another tear, 'We said he had a gift, that dog, should have been called Romeo, he brought me and my Phyllis together. And the young girl that found him, well she was helped by a passer-by to get our Roddy out of the river. They married the next year. Yes, even in death he knew when two people were made for each other.'

Peter smiled and looked at Isobel. She smiled back at him, her cheeks flushed. He reached out and took hold of her hand.

Outside in the garden a dog barked.

A Different Time, a Different Life

The lights were dimmed as the last remaining members of staff at the gallery left for the night. She took one final look around to check everything was in order and being satisfied it was, she joined the others to head to the pub for an after-work drink. She wondered if Lance from the maintenance department would be there this evening. He never seemed to notice her, but she sure had noticed him! What a hunk! She skipped down the road after her friends in a hopeful mood.

The door of the gallery was now closed. All was quiet, all was still, save for the soft sound of lapping water from the far end of gallery fourteen. She sat in the boat, watching and waiting. Her eyes scanned the room in the darkness as they became accustomed to the half-light.

She knew tonight was her last chance to see him, for tomorrow she would be taken back to her home gallery. This exhibition to which she had been brought had at last included the love of her life and maybe this time her passion and adoration of him will not end in such sorrow! Maybe he will notice her.

Her long golden hair cascaded down onto her ivory linen dress. Her sad soulful eyes looked down as she moved gracefully out of the boat and into the gallery. Taking one lighted candle from the prow of the vessel, she stepped down from the canvas and placed her damp bare feet onto the floor. The river mist that clung to her hair glistened in the candlelight. The long sleeves of her dress dripped river water onto the wooden flooring, leaving droplets like sparkling jewels. She knew he wasn't far away and moved silently past the other exhibits. She glanced at some of the other paintings on display. So many wonderful creations of tragic females locked in infinity. She had been given her moment of eternity too; she was Elaine, the Lady of Shalott. Her creator had captured her, as she was about to float downstream to Camelot, in the final moments of her life.

But now, here she was, moving silently in the art gallery, getting another chance to gaze upon her heart's desire – her Lancelot! She continued carefully along the gallery, making no sound. She knew she had to get to him, see if he felt the same. She glided along the floor, her heart beating wildly in her chest, her face aglow with excitement.

She thought back to her time in the tower and the moment when she first saw his reflection in the mirror. She was hypnotized by his beauty! How handsome and wonderful he looked on his magnificent horse. She saw his jet-black hair framing his heavenly face. He seemed to glow in the sunlight. Astride his steed, he rode past in full armour that had flickered and sparkled in the rays of the sun into her mirror.

From that moment, she knew that even though she was cursed, cursed to never cast her eyes on Camelot, her life would be futile and not worth a single breath more if she could not look upon his face again. He had captivated her. So, she left her tower and amongst the willows she found a boat to sail down towards Camelot. It was at this moment in time that she had been held, captured by the artist. And now, her chance had arrived. She knew another artist had caught Lancelot in an instant of his life and this work was also hanging in the gallery.

He was a heartbeat away.

She saw him. He was sleeping. He was half sitting with his sword in his hand. His shield was hanging on a bush whilst his horse stood behind, waiting for him obediently. She held the candle up higher so she could see his face.

In hushed tones, she said, 'If only he would wake, if only I could hear the sweet words from his lips.'

She saw a slight flickering of his long dark lashes. His hand tightened on the hilt of his sword. She watched in anticipation, willing his eyes to open further.

She licked her rosebud lips and sighed, 'Oh my love, my precious love, I would that you awaken for me so I may end my days remembering this wonderful moment.'

His dark eyes slowly opened. He smiled and took in a long deep breath. Stretching and standing up he looked across to her.

'Good evening my Lady,' he said and reaching out to her trembling form, he took her hand and held her soft delicate fingers within his own and slowly stepped across the frame onto the gallery floor beside her.

He took the candle from her and placing it on the floor, held both her hands.

'My Lady of Shalott, I am truly honoured that you seek me out. Let us talk of days gone by and of Arthur and Camelot.'

So overcome with her love for him was she, that her eyes were brimming with salty tears, about to cascade onto her cheeks. He put his hand onto her chin and raised her head to look at her. He wiped the tears from her face and looked into her eyes that were full of love for him.

'Why do you cry so, sweet lady?'

She met his gaze, 'My dear Lancelot, I have dreamt of this moment for so long, ever since I glimpsed you in my mirror in my cursed tower. I took a boat to sail to Camelot so that I might see you, touch you, hear your voice, but it was not to be.'

His long dark hair fell forward as he lowered his head, 'Come, let us sit awhile,' he whispered.

They sat on the hard wooden floor of the gallery, the candle still burning beside them. He put his arm around her and pulled her toward him slightly. He could smell the sweet scent of wild flowers in her hair as she rested her head upon his shoulder. He pushed her hair back and kissed her neck gently.

'I am so sorry sweet lady. In a different time, different life, we could be together but this heart is promised to another. The Lady Guinevere is where my heart resides.'

The tears slowly made their way down her cheeks. All this time she had waited, but it had been in vain.

'Please do not be sad. You are a most beautiful woman. Your hair is like tendrils of spun gold, your lips full and red and your eyes, at this moment, they are like overflowing pools of crystal clear springs.' He took hold of her hand and stroked her long elegant fingers, 'I am sure whoever casts their eyes upon you are transfixed with your beauty, as am I.'

'My Lord, I thank you for your honesty and I can at least continue my existence knowing I have heard your sweet voice and will remember your touch for an eternity.'

He leant across to her, 'And also remember my kiss.' He kissed her mouth, her face, her neck. They sat in silence, in the candlelight, holding each other close, knowing they had only this time and soon they would be locked in their own worlds again.

The candle flickered, the dried wax spread out like fingers on the floor and then the flame was no more. The darkness surrounded them, the two souls from another time.

She had to go back. She knew that she couldn't stay away from her canvas for too long but it wrenched at her heart to know she was going to have to say goodbye.

She turned to him, holding his arms, looking at him pleadingly, 'Take me with you. You have your horse, we could ride wherever we desire!'

'You know that our destiny has already been decided, in this life it cannot be so. But do not forget, we may have our chance in a different time, a different life. Hold onto that.' He pulled her to her feet and held her tightly to him, breathing in her skin, the smell of her hair. 'We must go our separate ways now, but when our souls meet again I will know you. I will be transfixed by your beauty yet again, of that I have no doubt.'

They heard the sound of the river lapping against the side of her boat from along the gallery. His horse began to snort, getting restless without its master. It was time to go. With one last look into each other's eyes they parted. He climbed up and sat down within the canvas, eyes flickering slowly shut. Asleep, caught in a moment.

She gasped, stifled a sob and ran back to her place in the gallery. Turning one last time to look towards where her love lay sleeping and then she stepped up and was back into the boat. She sat with hand on the chain about to set the vessel free. Ready to float away, caught in a moment.

She came into the gallery early as she had a busy day ahead. It was the end of the exhibition. Each canvas had to be ready and carefully wrapped to be sent back to whoever had loaned them for display.

She stopped and sniffed. What was that she could smell? Smoke? No, can't be, the alarm would have sounded. She shook her head thinking she was imagining things. Heading along the length of the room she noticed something solid and white on the floor. What on earth was that? She peered down and looked closely at the hardened candle wax. She made a mental note to have words with the cleaner, who obviously hadn't done her job properly. Goodness knows how that got there in the first place.

She walked briskly along and suddenly her foot slid and she nearly slipped on the wet floor. There was a fairly large puddle of rather rancid smelling water on the floor in front of the Lady of Shalott. She looked up to the ceiling for signs of a leak, it all looked fine. She looked again at the water. If it wasn't so bizarre she would have sworn there was duckweed amongst the huge puddle. She frowned, it was likely to start damaging the wood flooring if she didn't address the problem soon.

Her frown suddenly turned into a huge grin. She knew what that meant she could do!

She tapped in the number, 'Hello? Is that housekeeping? Elaine here, is Lance about by any chance? Good, can you ask him to come down to gallery fourteen ASAP? Got a leak or something odd going on.' She put the phone away and smiled to herself, rather pleased that she had an excuse to see Lance again.

He had been at the pub last night. She thought things between them might have turned a corner. He had smiled at her across the table but then Malcolm from the ticket office dragged him off to play pool so that was the end of that.

Her stomach somersaulted as she heard footsteps outside getting closer. The door to the gallery swung open and he stood in the doorway looking across at her. He found it hard to move for he was transfixed by her beauty.

Be Careful What You Wish For

Karen sat in front of the dressing table mirror not liking what she saw. She was sixty-five. How did that happen? Where had all the time gone? Her fingers touched the necklace that Bernard had hung around her neck that morning. It was a beautiful gift, so intricately worked. He had bought it from the new-age shop in their local Surrey town where they sold lots of ethnic style jewellery. This piece looked as if it was African in origin. The front was covered with fine strands of a silver metal twisted and intertwined with small silver leaves. From behind the vegetation, eyes made from small chips of tiger's eye stone stared out at her, giving the necklace a magical but slightly sinister feel. Bernard had assured it was fair trade so hopefully some small child in a sweat shop hadn't strained her eyes to make this beautiful piece.

  She leant closer to the mirror and ran her fingers across her skin. The lines were increasing daily. She recalled the holidays where her skin had glistened in the sunshine, when she could run across the sand without her knees giving out. Sixty-five and what had she done with her life? They say it's the things you didn't do in your life that you regret when you are old. There were so many things she wished she had done. If only she could turn back the clock and live it all again, wouldn't that just be great? She wished she was a child again.

  Her hand reached up and held her head as she was suddenly seized by a sharp pain in her skull. The spark of life that lived within the body of Karen floated upwards and was swept away in the breeze. It rose up into another dimension where time has no beginning or end. It waited.

In flat thirty-three on the top floor of the tower block on the outskirts of Glasgow, Tanya was helping her mother. She was only twelve years old but this was the second baby she'd help deliver. The flat was over crowded with her and six sisters and now another baby was arriving. Her Pa had gone to phone for an ambulance but he'd been gone over an hour. Tanya knew he would be in the pub, already wetting the baby's head.

The baby held back before it made its final push, pausing until the spark of consciousness that had been waiting, came to rest inside the new life.

Tanya heard the door slam shut some hours later and her father staggered home. Her mother looked down at her new child, a boy at last. They would call him Daniel after her dad. Maybe her husband would allow her some rest from childbirth now. She was weary. She looked at her new son and his sweet face, so innocent and she despaired for his future.

Daniel was playing football in the park in the nicer side of town. He spent most of his days outside, he hated the flat, hated his life. Why did he have to be born into such a poor family? He looked across at the big houses that lined one side of the park. They had huge bay windows and granite steps up to wooden front doors. No out of order lifts and eleven flights of stairs for their occupants. He kicked the football hard, releasing his anger. It rolled across the footpath towards the road. As he ran to retrieve it, his last thought was how he wished he lived with a rich family. The car hit him with great force.

The spark of life floated away. Eventually it came to rest as Caroline Smyth gave birth to Justin, her second son, at Queen Charlotte's hospital in London.

Justin had lived his first seven years at home with his parents and younger siblings but had known that the time would come that he would have to go away to boarding school. It was what his older brother Jeremy had done and it was, without question, something he would do too. He had done his best with his lessons but he knew it wasn't going to be enough for his father who wanted Justin to follow in his footsteps and be a lawyer. Justin had tried to tell him it wasn't something he wanted to do but he never listened.

Justin headed off to the rugby field and watched as Harry made everyone laugh with his jokes. Harry, a tall lad, built like an ox, was a popular boy at the school. Justin never felt part of the team. He felt like an outsider. The game started and his stomach began to knot. He hated sport, really feared rugby. He wasn't strong enough or able enough to cope with the game. There was the sound of a whistle as the London to Bristol train went speeding along the track in the distance. That was something he'd love to do. Just sit and drive a train across great fields of green, through towns and cities. He stood on the field and began to daydream. How he would love to do a job like that. Justin, lost in his thoughts, was unaware of Harry getting closer. Wanting to get the ball, Harry had pushed him out of his way, his arm landing an almighty blow to Justin's head. It was as Justin was wishing he could be a train driver that he fell to the ground.

The spark of life floated high into the sky waiting for its next host. It finally reached its destination in London and made itself at home just as baby Gerard was born.

Gerard would be glad to be home. The track between London and Dover had lost its appeal. It was boring. The same route day after day. When he'd first taken the job, he had thought it would be exciting being in charge of a speeding train but now it was just another job. Boring. He found his mind wandered and he didn't always concentrate as much as he should. That was why he couldn't stop in time when the woman jumped from the bridge. He flew out from the cab, his heart banging in his chest. He had looked down at her mangled corpse on the track and quickly shut his eyes. He felt the bile rise in his throat. Even with his eyes closed he could still see the horrific vision of what he had done. He wished he was blind then he would never had seen the bloody mess, would never have been a train driver in the first place and caused this poor woman's death. It was just as he had a massive heart attack at the edge of the track that the spark of life floated out and headed off on its next journey.

In a small village in Kenya a little girl is born and the spark of life picks out this little baby as its next host. Her father chooses her name. He calls her Mbura. She lives a poor existence and unlike her eight siblings isn't as able to help her mother with the chores. Mbura's mother had contracted rubella when she had been pregnant and so Mbura had been born blind. She grows into a very beautiful child. She never complains. Her parents know she is special. The wise man of the village tells them that Mbura has special powers. She may not have her own vision but he says she has the power to help others see the things that they are blind to in their own lives. A charitable organisation arrives in the area to help struggling families and they find Mbura a place in a workshop making jewellery. Even though she has no vision her other senses are acute and her fingers have great sensitivity. She is able to feel the metal and stones under her skin and deftly craft out some beautiful necklaces to be sold in the western world.

Mbura sat in the workshop and listened as the charity organiser praised her work, telling her how beautiful her products were. Mbura was used to being blind, it was all she had ever known but felt so sorry that she could not glance upon the jewellery she had produced and see if it really was as beautiful as she was being told. It made her feel sad that she would never see her work, or see her parents. She had a moment of self-pity and wished she had never been born.

Karen opened her eyes. She is in a hospital bed. Bernard is sitting by her side. He had been worried, he told her. They thought they had lost her but somehow, she had fought for her life and was recovering well. He leant over and kissed her.

She smiles at him, so grateful for her life. She asks that the next time he comes to visit would he bring her the necklace he had bought her for her birthday. He looks at her quizzically. He never bought her a necklace.

The Other Woman

Rosie emptied the rubbish into the bin and made her way back to the house. She squinted as the sun glinted on the bedroom window. Was that movement upstairs? Maybe Dan was already home. Opening the back door, she called his name. The house was silent. She shrugged. It must have been a trick of the light. She climbed the stairs and went into the bathroom. She'd have time for a quick shower before Dan got home from work and then she could get started on the evening meal.

The hot needles of water felt good on her aching shoulders. She'd been off work with a nasty virus and her muscles were still aching and sore. The doctor had assured her it was normal but she had hoped she would have felt a lot better by now. She was due to go back to work the following week but wondered how she'd cope, she felt so tired all the time.

Rosie wandered into the bedroom, glancing at her naked body in the mirror, she stood and studied it with despair. Her ribs showed so clearly now, her thighs no longer firm, her skin looked too loose on her arms. She sighed as she rubbed the towel across her damp skin. Glancing back to her reflection she caught sight of a shadow, a whisper of movement on the landing, she turned quickly but there was nothing to be seen.

She was tired, it was making her imagine things. Looking at the clock it was only a few minutes after four, she had time for a nap. She slid under the covers and within minutes was in a deep sleep.

'You're home at last Dan! You've worked late today, you must be so tired,' the woman said.

Dan smiled at her, giving her his sexy smile and then kissed the woman full on the lips. The woman turned, her hands caressing her swelling belly.

'How's my baby today?' Dan asked, resting his head against their child growing within the woman's body.

'Don't worry, the baby is just fine,' the woman laughed and grabbed his hand, pulling him towards the bed.

Rosie lay still. She watched the scene unfold. Why did she keep having this dream? She tried to push it from her subconscious mind. Rosie forced her eyelids to open just at the point where the woman pulled Dan onto the bed. She didn't want to dream this. Didn't want to dream about her husband making love with another woman. A woman who could give him the child that had eluded them. Rosie felt the mattress dip, felt movement beside her as Dan and the woman laughed and fell onto the bed.

Rosie sat up. She was alone.

The doctor signed her off for another week.

'These viruses take time to shift. Just rest and drink plenty of fluids. Come back and see me Friday,' he had said with his gaze fixed firmly on the computer monitor.

She didn't feel hungry anymore. The ravenous appetite that had taken hold a few weeks ago had disappeared. Not that it had done her any good. Her weight was still dropping.

Her friend Amanda came to see her.

'Rosie! Go back to the doctor, see a different one if needs be, but get it sorted. You're going to fade away. How do you feel in yourself? Still tired?'

'Yes, very tired. These dreams aren't helping. They feel so real when I wake up, almost as if I hadn't been sleeping at all.'

Amanda picked up the telephone handset and pushed it towards her friend, 'Ring the surgery,' she ordered, 'now!'

She had three days to wait before she could see the head doctor at the practice. Amanda had taken the phone from her when she realised her friend was being fobbed off with a locum. Amanda had been strong and assertive, everything Rosie didn't have the strength to be anymore. The receptionist had finally given in and made the appointment for her. Dr Roberts had a good reputation.

The next day Rosie slept through the alarm. When she did awake, the house was silent. She put her right hand across the bed, feeling for Dan. It was cold. He'd gone to work without waking her! She felt hurt. He'd never done that before.

The front door slammed shut.

'Dan!' she cried out and ran across the landing to the front bedroom and peered down to the path. Her stomach knotted as she witnessed Dan and the woman together, holding hands as they walked towards the gate.

Rosie banged on the window.

'Dan! Dan!' she called. But they didn't hear her as they headed towards the park together.

The door swung open.

'Did you call?' Dan asked, his chin white with foam, mid shave.

She ran over to him and hugged him tight allowing the shaving soap to cover her cheek.

'I thought I saw you...just now...with a blonde woman.'

He took her hand and led her back to their bedroom.

'Come on, get back into bed, you're getting cold,' he settled down next to her under the duvet.

Holding her hand tightly he looked at her with concern, 'Come on Rosie, tell me what you thought you saw. Is it the same woman you dream I am kissing?'

She nodded.

'Describe this mystery woman to me.'

'Well, she has long blonde hair and she is pregnant,' Rosie sobbed.

Dan pulled her to him, 'Oh Rosie, is this what it's all about? I really don't mind that we can't have kids you know. It's you I want. I want you and no one else.'

'So, who is she? Why do I keep seeing her? Maybe I'm seeing a ghost.'

'Well I'm unlikely to be having an affair with a ghost, now am I? And a blonde one at that. No way! It's only redheads for me!' he said as his fingers ran through her auburn locks.

It was the day before she was due to go back to see the specialist for her results. Dr Roberts had referred her to the hospital for tests. He said not to worry but the look on his face had told Rosie he was concerned.

She was finding it hard to keep food down now and she just wanted to know for sure. In her heart, she knew what they would say. She looked out of the window at the garden. The daffodil bulbs were just starting to show through. She wondered if she would get to see them in flower. She began to daydream, imagining the garden in full bloom, seeing it how she loved it, so full of colour.

It was then that the baby started to cry. She peered out of the window into the next-door garden. Maybe they had visitors? But there was no-one to be seen. The crying became louder. It was coming from the front of the house.

Rosie walked quietly towards the cries. She stood at the door of the front bedroom and gasped. The woman was sitting on a chair by a cot. She had a baby in her arms and was just about to feed it.

'There, there, little one. Here's your milk. Is that nice?' the woman spoke softly to the child.

'Who are you and what are you doing in my house?' Rosie said.

The woman turned her face to the doorway and frowned before turning her attention back to feeding the baby.

It was obvious she couldn't see Rosie but she had heard something. Rosie stood transfixed as the woman continued to breast feed the baby and then gathered it up, holding it against her chest, its head above her shoulder. She rubbed its back and walked around the room, kissing the child's hair before standing to look out of the window. The baby's eyes fixed onto Rosie and looked directly at her. It smiled and started to make happy gurgling noises.

The woman continued to talk to the baby, 'I'm looking out for your daddy. He should come home from work soon my darling,' she kissed the baby again. 'Your mummy and daddy both love our little Rosie,' she said.

Rosie held onto the door frame. Her head began to spin and her legs collapsed from under her.

Dan had found her lying on the landing. She was only in a nightdress and her skin was icy to the touch. He'd wrapped her in a blanket and carried her to the bed, holding her tight, sharing the warmth of his body.

She was still very weak when they sat in the specialist's office the next day. He had sat at his desk, a kind smile on his face. She watched as his lips wrestled with the words he had to say. She only caught snatches of sentences. He was sorry. Too late to do anything.
 She looked across at Dan whose face was wet with tears and reached out her hand to him. They both stood up and went home. He held her tightly that night, telling her he would never ever love anyone as much as he loved her. He cried into the nape of her neck, begging her not to leave him.

Dan tried to keep the funeral a cheerful affair as requested by Rosie. Everyone should be in bright colours and happy songs were to be sung, she had said. Dan looked around at the congregation. So many friends and neighbours had come along to pay their respects. Even Wendy, the widow of the man who had been in the next room to Rosie at the hospice had attended. Over the past few weeks they had shared their sadness at the impending loss of their partners over coffee. Rosie had touched so many people's lives with her happy and cheerful personality. He would do his best to remember her how she was most of her life and not the sad and thin woman she had been at the end, sleepy and weak and having dreams and hallucinations that caused her so much grief.

Four years on and he still felt Rosie's presence in the house, he enjoyed feeling that she was close by. He would smell her perfume or for a brief second glimpse her reflection in the mirror. He sometimes felt the warmth of her body in the bed. He could never leave this house. He could never leave Rosie. Wendy understood. She didn't mind sharing him with his wife's ghost. Wendy knew that he would never love her as he had loved Rosie. Just as she'd never love Dan as much as she had loved her husband. But they did love each other. Enough to get married and to have the baby that they both yearned for. They named her Rosie.

Bluebell Wood

As the new day began to filter through the gaps in the skylight she awoke. A thrush began to sing its morning melody from the top of the ash tree outside. She glanced across at her partner. He was sound asleep in the land of dreams. She thought back to their arrival at the campsite and her excitement at seeing the woods alongside the entrance track. The trees stood in a carpet of blue. She had opened the campervan window and breathed in the intoxicating sweet perfume of the bluebells. Robert had reluctantly agreed that on the morning of their departure they would find time to walk the woods and enjoy the springtime spectacle of blue.

As she now lay in the van she checked the time. It was only 5am but she couldn't push the idea from her head. It would be so nice to walk in the woods with the dawn chorus echoing amongst the trees whilst she enjoyed the amazing sight of the sea of flowers around her feet.

Beside her Robert stirred briefly, then turned onto his side, deep asleep. The lure of the bluebells and birdsong was too much to resist and so she slipped out of the bed, put on her jeans, pulled a thick jumper over her head and taking the spare keys, stepped out into the early morning light.

She stopped a moment. Should she have left a note, letting him know where she was heading but dismissed the thought. She knew him well enough to know he would sleep for many an hour yet. He'd not miss her.

The air was full of sweet voices. So many birds greeting a new dawn. The rain from the previous evening had passed but had left a cloak of green richness across the trees and fields. She breathed in the fresh new day.

The campsite behind her, she took the path into the wood. A blackbird raised the alarm as she walked along, afraid she was danger but soon realising she was no threat it began to rejoice at the sun-rise with its liquid song.

As she ventured deeper into the wood she began to relax, feeling the freedom of the place, somewhere she wasn't ruled by time or commitments. Things had been difficult between her and

Robert for some months and it felt good to be away from his critical words and sour face.

The wood closed in around her and her senses soon located the heavy scent of the bluebells. The smell was intoxicating and her feet raced her along the path towards the perfume. It wasn't long before the canopy of trees embraced an ocean of blue stretching out to her right. Taking a narrow path alongside a holly bush she made her way into the dell of flowers.

Her arms outstretched to her sides, eyes heavenwards she began to spin around, laughing with joy, feeling the moment, before dropping breathless to the ground. As she sat amongst the bluebells she was unaware of eyes amongst the greenery - watching. Staying hidden, unsure of her intentions, the eyes watched as she sat smiling to herself. A thrush began its morning rhapsody and she lay back amongst the flowers and shut her eyes. The breeze picked up and carried the shiny bright dust through the air, finally stopping above her dozing form. She smiled to herself in her sleepy state as the fine powder trickled down and gently caressed her skin.

As she slept they began to emerge from the bushes and return to their celebrations. The woman had disturbed them but now she slept peacefully and they could continue with their festivities. Their delicate fingers entwined, they began to dance around in a circle amongst the bluebells, singing as they skipped with joy. Some of the younger ones broke free and pulled the bells from a few of the older blooms and laughed as they placed them onto their heads, wearing them as hats. They darted across to the woman and looked closely at her. She had a kind face they decided. A young man with beautiful golden hair crouched down beside the stranger. He reached out his long fingers and touched her brow. He felt her sadness, could sense her desire to escape from the world in which she lived.

She was aware of his hands on her skin and slowly her eyelids fluttered open and found she was looking at the most beautiful face she had ever seen. His deep turquoise eyes looked back at her as he smiled. She smiled back and then a dozen more faces appeared around her. Beautiful young women and small angelic looking children.

'Hello,' she said and they all jumped back in fright as she spoke.

The man edged forward again, 'You can see us?' he asked in amazement.

She nodded and laughed, 'Of course I can. Why shouldn't I?'

A young woman stepped forward, braver than the rest and replied, 'We do not mix with humans. We usually just watch you from afar. It is only at dusk and dawn that we come openly into the woods, the rest of the time we keep hidden from view.'

'Why? Why do you have to keep away?'

'Do you not know who we are?' the brave girl asked. 'The fact you can see us shows you have the second sight, that you could become one of us if you so wished.'

She sat up and looked at them. Become one of them? But who were they? They were all so beautiful and so happy. It was the happiness that shone from their faces that made her envy them. They seemed carefree and light - just how she wished her life could be. A swift thought passed through her mind momentarily. Could she stay here and not go back to Robert? Her eyes took in the faces of the cheerful souls that surrounded her. They looked so mystical. The thread of their dresses were so fine they could have been spun with gossamer. They were barefoot and the children with their rosebud lips wore cute little blue hats, just like bluebell flowers, perched upon their curls. Her heart missed a beat. They were bluebell flowers! But how could that be? They would have to be tiny to wear the flowers as hats but they were the same size as her! She rubbed her eyes and looked around. Yes, she was still sitting amongst the bluebells but no longer were the flowers around her feet, they now towered above her. What had happened to her? Was she dreaming?

Afraid, she jumped up, 'What have you done to me?' she cried.

The young man came closer to her, 'Don't be scared. The sleeping dust made you small so we could feel safe. We will let you go but first you must drink this,' he held out an acorn cup filled with a sweet-smelling liquid.' Don't worry it won't hurt you. It's not hemlock.'

'Hemlock? Would that hurt me?'

He nodded his head, 'We rarely use it, only if we feel strongly that someone had wronged one of our own. And anyway, we wouldn't make you drink it, we usually use poison darts. Once it hits the back of the neck, our enemies trouble us no more.'

'So ...why do I have to drink this?' she asked.

'Once you drink the liquid you will be your full size again and will forget you have ever seen us...unless of course you wish to stay?'

She glanced around as the eyes of the fairies watched her, waiting to see if she would drink. She lifted the cup to her lips and hesitated, looked again at the handsome man who was still smiling at her.

She lowered the cup, 'Can I really stay?'

The children giggled and clapped their hands and the young man kissed her cheek, 'Welcome to the world of the Fae. We were all hoping you would decide to stay with us. Our little family needs new bloodlines to keep us strong. Hopefully we will continue to live and thrive within these woods now that you will become one of us.'

'So if I join you, will I stay small - forever?' she asked.

'Yes, you will, but your body will remain in the human world for a year and a day so if you change your mind we can return your soul back to your human form,' he looked into her eyes, 'Are you sure?'

She nodded.

He grasped her hand and pulled her to her feet and she joined the faeries as they formed a circle and danced and danced and danced....

Robert had raised the alarm when he had awoken and realised after an hour or so that something had happened to her. At first, he assumed she had gone to see the bluebells. He was relieved really as he couldn't care less about the bloody flowers. He just wanted to get to the next campsite and go and meet up with his friend and look around the steam train museum. They had a rare locomotive on display but it was heading to a museum up north in a day or two. He didn't want to miss seeing it. When she didn't turn up he became angry. She was going to delay them now. After a few hours, he went to the site office and asked if they'd seen her. It was then that the woman in the neighbouring caravan appeared, flushed faced with her dog.

'Your wife! I have just seen her lying amongst the bluebells in the wood. I tried to wake her but she just won't stir! You must come!'

Robert sighed. What was the matter with her now? Had she fallen asleep? His unfeeling heart had a brief moment of compassion when it crossed his mind that maybe she'd been attacked. That would really delay them! They'd have to get the police involved then.

Accompanied by one of the site wardens, he followed the dog walking woman back into the wood to where his wife lay.

They edged their way past the holly bush and into the bluebell dell. Robert leant down and shook his wife's arms.

'Tanny, wake up, come on woman,' he shouted at her.

The dog walker glanced at the warden and they shared a look of horror at his lack of care or love for his wife.

He shook her again and slowly her eyes fluttered opened and looked at him with blank eyes, 'Who are you?' she mumbled and began singing quietly to herself.

They tried to get through to her but she was in some kind of daze and wouldn't move from the woods. Robert reluctantly agreed that a doctor be called who on examining Titania, declared that she had suffered some sort of mental trauma and needed a stay in hospital. The dog walker and site warden made their way back to the campsite to keep watch out for the ambulance, leaving the doctor with Titania. They glanced across at Robert who stood by an aging oak tree on the path, its snake-like roots interspersed with huge cavernous holes at his base. He held his mobile phone to his ear.

The dog walker mumbled to the site warden as they headed back, 'I should think living with him is what gave her the mental trauma.'

Keen to get on the road, Robert chatted to his fellow steam train enthusiast friend letting him know of the hold-up, 'So, I should be with you in about two hours. I won't bother waiting for the ambulance - this old quack can sort Tanny out. She won't know I'm gone - she's away with the fairies,' he laughed.

He put the phone in his pocket and headed back, not giving his wife a second glance. As he walked along the path he felt a sharp prick in his skin and brought his hand up to the back of his neck.

'Pesky insects,' he said before falling to the ground dead.

A small hand pulled a curtain of moss across the hole at the base of the oak and the sound of female laughter disappeared below the woodland floor

An Inconvenient Truth

I glanced sideways under lowered lashes at my mother and watched as her lips mumbled the words along with the rest of the congregation. Her fingers grabbed at each bead in turn, the silver crucifix making its circular journey once more.

'Holy Mary, Mother of God, pray for us sinners.'

Where had it got her? All these years life had been a struggle but still she clung onto that rosary as if they were some sort of magic beads. The whole thing was just like a bloody pantomime. But to her God was the truth, she believed in it all and said we both needed to pray extra hard for forgiveness and pray for my father's soul. But I couldn't do it anymore. It was time to move on. I knew she would get upset, tell me I would end up in hell if I left the church. The brain washing had Mum believing that everyone meets their maker and it depended on our sins in life if we end up in Heaven, Purgatory or Hell. But I don't believe in Hell, or Heaven or any of the old tosh they feed the masses to try and keep us in check. When you're dead you're dead. Anyway, I've already seen hell. That's why I've decided it is time to head off. I'm going to enjoy life. I'm twenty-three, too bloody old to be living at home with my widowed Mum.

I told her that evening. She was wiping up the Sunday tea service. The Royal Albert set. It was always brought out on a Sunday. Bread and butter tea with the bone china. She had looked at me as if I had told her the world had ended. The cup fell from her hands, shattering into pieces over the smart tiled floor. I looked into her eyes and saw that her heart had shattered too.

'But you can't leave. Where will you go? Your job? You've got your job at the dairy.'

'I've handed in my notice Mum. I leave on Friday. I've got to go. I want to live my life.'

She knelt down and began to gather up the broken pieces of crockery.

'My beautiful cup, all these years I've looked after it and now see what's happened,' she leant across to pick up a jagged piece that had fallen under the cupboard. Her knee found a sharp edge of broken china and she cried out, 'Oh see what you've made me do,' she wailed and fell back onto her bottom and began to cry.

'Mum, please don't be upset,' I crouched down next to her but she pulled away from my touch and began to dab at her knee with a tissue.

I jumped up and moistened a piece of kitchen towel, 'Here let me help Mum.' I began to wipe at her knee, making sure there wasn't anything still stuck in the wound. Looking after her as I've always done. Supporting her after Dad's death ten years ago. I squatted down and put my arm around her. She continued to cry. Softly now, long lines of tears made their way slowly down her cheeks.

'I'm sorry Mum. It's all decided. I've got myself a job down in London. I've found a flat share too.'

She nodded, 'I knew you'd want to go one day. You've spent too long looking out for your old mum,' she grabbed my hand and looked at me, a look of despair on her face. 'You'll have to speak to Father O'Donnell. Tell him where you're going, he'll put you in touch with the parish priest. You have to keep going to Church. You must. Our Lord will forgive us if we show we recognise we are sinners.'

I nodded. I wouldn't tell her I was done with religion. Done with the priests. Where had Father O'Donnell been when Dad had been giving me a black eye or cracking Mum's ribs? The Father had known what had been happening. Dad, ever the good Catholic had given his confession and then headed to the social club to down more pints to fuel him for his next act of domestic violence.

Thirteen years old I'd been. The day I grew up. The day I took a life. I couldn't bear it anymore. My whole life had been a constant battle ground. My earliest memory was standing up in my cot watching him slap her round the face. As I got older I would try to shield her, goad him on so he would hit me rather than see her hurt.

That last time I'd been out on my paper round so he had got to Mum before I could act as a barrier. I'd walked in through the back door and Mum had her back to me. She was filling the teapot with boiling water, making him a cup of tea. Dad was sitting up to the table, his skinny body clad in a string vest and his pants. His cigarette hanging between his lips as he scanned the newspaper, deciding what horse to back. It looked like an ordinary family scene until Mum turned around. I saw her face. One eye was shut tight, her brow was swollen like a huge plum. Her lip was still bleeding. She lifted the teapot awkwardly with her left hand and I could tell by the way she held her right arm close to her body that he had broken her wrist again.

I saw red. I couldn't stand it anymore. The boiling tea was the first weapon I used. That put him off guard as he yelled and cussed, jumping up from his seat to get to the sink to splash cold water onto his burning genitals.

'You wait boy,' he growled as he stood with his back to me, trying to get as much water onto his scalding flesh. That was his downfall. He didn't see me lift the copper pan from the stove, lift it high and swing it across his head. He was unconscious for days. Mum said we must visit him, that I mustn't show my feelings otherwise they wouldn't believe our story that it had been a terrible accident. I hated sitting by his bedside playing the loving son. Father O'Donnell had come in to see my father the once, it was when the doctor had told us that it didn't look hopeful that Dad would survive. He'd given the last rites and then turned to me.

'I'm always around Marty if you ever want to talk. Do not forget our Lord forgives sinners.'

I think that was when I finally made up my mind what a load of nonsense it all was. We are born, we live, we die. The end. So, I didn't worry about what I did anymore, I wasn't going to Hell, in fact the opposite, I'd just released Mum and me out of our own hell.

Dad regained consciousness briefly, I had been sitting by the bed reading a magazine. Mum had gone off to get a cup of tea from one of the machines on the floor below. I was engrossed in an article about the latest computer game, being released that Christmas when I heard his laboured breathing as he tried to speak.

'Marty,' a voice full of phlegm called to me.

I peered over the magazine and looked at him lying on the bed. His eyes were closed. I leant across and looked down at his still form. His eyes shot open and he stared at me. I saw hatred in those eyes as he spoke his final words before he took his last breath.

'I'll see you in Hell son.'

The day I set off for London was a foggy November day. I promised Mum I would be home to see her at Christmas. Her eyes had filled with tears as she watched me put on my coat and hook the straps of my backpack across my shoulders.

'I best go, I don't want to miss the train.'

'Don't forget to ring me when you get there,' she said, straightening the collar on my new black overcoat. She grabbed my hand and I felt her shove something around my fingers. Her rosary.

'Mum, no. It's yours. You keep it.'

'I know you doubt the Lord. But please take it - for me. Promise me you'll go to Mass,' she pleaded.

I nodded. Let her think there is a God looking out for me, if it makes her happy.

I kissed her and hugged her tight and was soon striding along the road heading for the railway station. I'd been waiting for this moment for so long. I'd spent so much of my life looking out for Mum. It was great to have a sense of freedom at last. The fog kept an icy chill in the air and so as I began to cross the road, I tucked my hands deep in my pockets. My fingers felt the beads of the rosary Mum had pushed upon me. The muted headlights of the bus came out from nowhere. I felt the impact before the fog closed in around me and everything went black.

I could feel the heat from the flames on my naked flesh before I opened my eyes and then I heard his voice.

'Hello son. I've been waiting for you.'

The Black Horse Ghost

They say the Pub is haunted. The locals tell holiday makers that the ghost of a woman walks at night. She is looking for her lover. The landlord smiles when he hears the stories but it seems to bring in extra custom so he doesn't mind. He doesn't believe the tales. Some people seem to enjoy being scared. The so called 'haunted' bedroom is where most people ask to sleep when they stay in the pub that sits high on the moor in the small village of Ellis Bell. The landlord's been at the Black Horse for nigh on ten years and in all that time he's not seen or sensed any spirits apart from the ones in the bottles behind his bar.

The villagers tell of people waking in the night and as they lay in the darkness they feel a heavy weight pressing onto their chest. They say it is the ghost of Emily as she constantly relives the moment she finds her betrothed in bed with the village whore. Her mind was so deranged by what she had discovered that she killed him as he lay hidden under the blankets. She stabbed him right through his heart, not realising it was his life she had taken. The blade had been destined for the whore.

The guest book of the Black Horse is filled with entries from visitors who tell how much they enjoyed their stay and yes, they did feel the presence of the ghost. Articles appear every few months in the local newspaper where people tell their tales of how they braved the haunted bedroom and witnessed orbs floating mysteriously around the room, voices screaming in the night and feeling pressure on their body as they lay in bed.

The landlord is happy with the publicity. He finds it amusing that people believe they are having these paranormal experiences. He thinks it is just suggestion that makes these people believe the room is haunted. They are just victims of their own over active imagination.

He is aware that there was a young woman called Emily who once played a part in the pub's history. He has seen her gravestone. It sits ravaged by time amongst the crumbling stones of the boundary wall of the churchyard on the edge of the village. It is a peaceful place, bordered by a drystone wall and an ancient yew in one corner with views across the fields beyond. The apple tree with its gnarled branches, bent and twisted with age, still stands by the lych gate but the mistletoe that grew on its branches is long gone. The landlord's wife feels a pang of guilt that her husband uses the poor woman's sad death to bring money to his business so she often lays flowers on the grave. She worries that Emily doesn't rest easy in the ground and hopes the flowers play a small part in obtaining forgiveness for her husband who doesn't believe in ghosts or life after death.

But he is wrong, he is the victim of his disbelief. He doesn't believe, so he will never see what really does walk his public house at night.

The locals think they know the story but I know the true tale. Let me tell you what really happened.

The man in the story was David, a local farmer and he had planned to marry Emily in the spring of 1875. Much of his time was spent at his farm and Emily saw him infrequently, especially so at harvest time but she was kept busy working at her father's public house. She was a friendly girl and was an asset to the Black Horse, her Father said. The customers liked her smile and would enjoy flirting with her but they knew she was promised to David and never crossed the line. That was until December 1874. Emily's Father had to go into York on business so Emily was left in charge. The bar was decorated with holly and hanging in the doorway was a sprig of mistletoe cut from the apple tree in the churchyard. At closing time the barman set off home to the village and Emily made ready to lock up for the night. But as she began to close the door she felt it being pushed open. Standing in the doorway was James, the son of Lord Thornton of Ellis Bell Manor.

'I'm not too late for a quick snifter am I Emily?' he sneered and pushed his way past her into the hostelry, 'Your Father is away I understand? Will you be safe here alone?' he said, as he put his hand up to her face, pinching her chin between his thumb and forefinger. 'A beautiful wench like you. I'd have thought all the men of the village would be around you like bees around a honey pot.'

Emily pulled away and moved closer to the door. From the smell of his breath she knew he had already been drinking and by the slurring of his words he had consumed a great deal. Her heart was thumping in her chest. She had to play this safe, she mustn't annoy him, but nor should she give reason to annoy his father who owned most of the land and properties in and around the village. Lord Thornton was also the local magistrate so would no doubt have her Father's licence revoked in an instant if she crossed him.

'I'm sorry Sir but we are shut. I'd lose my father's licence if I served you Sir. I know how much Lord Thornton doesn't abide law breakers and I wouldn't wish to annoy him. May I ask you leave, if you please Sir?' she gave a slight curtsey and opened the door.

He strode across to her, his face flushed with anger. He glanced up and noticed the mistletoe. Before she had a chance to step aside he grabbed her arms tightly and pressed his mouth roughly on her lips. She tried to push him away but he kicked the door shut and pressed her against the wall.

'You will find you do not wish to anger me either!' he spat and slapped her hard across her face. She fell sideways and lost her footing, banging her head on the corner of a table as she fell. She was vaguely aware of being carried across his shoulder and taken upstairs. He threw her onto the bed. Through a hazy blur of consciousness, she could feel his hands squeeze and pinch roughly at her flesh, could feel the searing pain between her legs, feel his hot breath on her face. The nausea rose in her throat and she tried to push him away but he punched at her face again and again rendering her unconscious.

She awoke. His breathing rattled out beside her and she tried to move. She tasted blood in her mouth and tried to edge herself out of the bed but the pain cut through her body and she lay still again. A crash echoed up from the bar as the main door banged shut and there were footsteps on the stairs. She was aware of her nakedness and pulled the blanket across her bruised and battered body and covered her face.

As David rushed into the bedroom his blind anger enveloped his mind. He didn't know what he would find. The barman had come to warn him that Emily may be in danger, for he had seen James approaching the Black Horse. David dashed over to the bed and whipped the covers away. His stomach muscles twisted in anguish. Emily's senses were so traumatised that her eyes did not recognise him and she let out a half sob and curled herself into a tight ball. David's fury swelled as he stood over James, who was out cold from the whiskey he had consumed to celebrate his victory. So, he was unaware of the blade as it punctured his skin.

Emily screamed. Blood gushed from James' mouth as his body arched with the first incision. Emily jumped up, pulling the blanket so to cover her body and cowered in the corner and watched as David plunged the blade into James' flesh again and again.

David finally saw the scene through more lucid eyes and stopped his frenzied attack. He stood and looked down at his blood sodden hands. The knife dropped from his fingers onto the bed next to the murdered rapist.

'Emily. Emily. It's alright now, you are safe,' he spoke softly as he edged his way slowly to his beloved as she sat trembling in the corner whimpering like an injured animal.

As he approached her she huddled closer to the wall, attempting to make distance between them.

'Emily? It's me. David,' he held out his arms, wanting to pull her close, hoping to comfort her.

'GET AWAY FROM ME,' she screamed, 'GET AWAY!' she jumped up and darted past him.

She dashed across to the bed and her fingers found the knife. She turned and stood holding the knife aloft, shouted at him, 'KEEP AWAY!'

Her manic screams were the last thing David heard. Her deranged eyes the last thing he saw.

No one ever knew the true story. The barman who had warned David had a good idea but couldn't tell the court the whole truth. Lord Thornton had made sure his son's part in the crime was never divulged. And so, Emily was hung for the murder of the man she was to have married. Yes, she had murdered him but if she'd had a fair trial she would have been deemed of unsound mind.

Buried just outside the churchyard her soul did not rest. It was not until she left her worldly body that clarity returned to her and she was aware of her actions. Her spirit has been in a state of unrest ever since. She sits by David's grave hoping he will return to her. She wanders the moors and visits her old bedroom in the Black Horse hoping to cross paths with the spirit of David. She needs to tell him she loves him.

So that is the true tale of the Black Horse ghost. And how do I know? I shall tell you how. For I am the one who waits in this peaceful churchyard. It has been me who sits by my beloved's gravestone waiting for him to return. But my waiting is over. And now after so many years I am able to tell my story, for it is time for me to go. The landlord will be sad as no longer people will tell their tales of ghosts and screams in the night. But I expect they will still think they hear and see me for that is the power of our imagination. The mind is a powerful tool. For me its power eventually did bear fruit and finally after well over a century David heard my cries.

We stood by our gravesides, separated only by the few stones still remaining from the boundary wall and we read the inscriptions. I touched his hand gently and he looked at me and smiled. He smiled because he could see my eyes and they were no longer the eyes of a demented mad woman.

'I love you David,' I whispered.

'And I you my darling Emily,' he looked down at the graves and rested his hand gently on my headstone. As he slowly faded from my sight, from his hand a blood red rose dropped and fell, landing on the soft earth between our graves. It was time to go.

The Forest Incident

June 2015

Claire called to Steve as she continued cycling ahead of him on the forest path, 'Come on slow coach. We really need to stop for our lunch soon.'

She stopped and propped up her bike and jumped onto a tree stump. Laughing, she watched him wobble up the steep sandy track towards her. His face was bright red, matching his hair.

She closed her eyes and held her face towards the sun enjoying its warmth on her skin. It was fun cycling in the forest but under the shade of the trees she had begun to feel chilly, now in the clearing she was able enjoy the brief spell of sunshine. But it didn't last for long as the ominous black clouds that had been threatening a downpour all morning closed in, shutting out its rays. No doubt the heavens would open soon. She hoped they wouldn't get too wet but as ever were prepared for all weathers with waterproofs in their back packs.

Steve finally arrived and took a long drink from his water bottle. He smiled at her and said, 'Did you want to eat lunch here?' then looking up at the darkening sky added, 'or do you want to go back to the van to have our lunch? Might save us getting soaked.'

Claire pulled face, 'I was hoping to get as far to the alleged landing site if we could and eat there. And by the looks of that sky we're going to get wet whatever we decide. At least the bad weather has grounded that helicopter today. I've found it unnerving flying nearby wherever we have been this holiday.'

'It's probably the RAF on some sort of training exercise I expect,' Steve said, trying to put to rest her fears that it was something more sinister. Although he had to admit it was spooky how it always seemed to be high above them at all the places they had visited so far.

'So, have you got the route map there, how much farther do we need to go?'

She pulled out the forestry commission's map and checked their position on the way marked route they were following, aptly named the UFO trail.

They had come to Suffolk for their summer break, staying in their camper van at the forest campsite. Being in school term time it was relatively quiet and they were able to walk and cycle along the woodland tracks without seeing another soul. They had chosen the forest as it was only a few hours from home and also because they were both interested in the incident that had supposedly happened there in 1980. When a UFO was reported to have landed and was seen by numerous military personnel. The local tourist department cashed in on this and had set up a trail through the forest with staging posts and information boards telling the story of the events thirty-five years previous.

Claire and Steve checked out their route and realising they were only a few minutes away from the alleged first landing site, they climbed back onto their bikes and headed on their way. Seconds later the leaden sky released its bounty and they pedalled as quickly as they could along the track.

As the deluge continued they rushed along finally reaching a crossroads in the paths. The right path opened to a small clearing overlooking farmland to the east, but they took the left track and under thundering skies soon found themselves at the entrance to the clearing where the first UFO sighting had taken place. They cycled into the area and Claire jumped down from her bike and swiftly pulled the waterproof jacket and trousers out from her rucksack.

'Quick Steve, come and shelter under the trees and get your waterproofs on,' she called to her husband as she stepped into the cumbersome over trousers.

They perched on the small wooden bench, both decked out in their waterproof clothing, hoods up over their heads as the rain slowly eased. With the water droplets dripping down onto their laps, they sat in silence as they took in the atmosphere of the place. Although the rain was subsiding, the sky was still charcoal grey and it felt more like dusk than midday. The sky was charged with the power of the elements and the thunder edged even closer. A flash of lightning suddenly lit up the replica space ship that had been positioned in the clearing by the Forestry commission. It had been made to match as close as possible the description by the serviceman who reported seeing it back in 1980. They had even added the strange hieroglyph type markings along the side of the replica craft.

Another crash of thunder bellowed around the forest and a crack of electrifying energy darted down onto the earth, lighting the sky as it ventured down from the heavens. The cattle in the nearby fields became spooked and began running across the field and calling out in distress.

3 a.m. December 1980

It had been a quiet watch at the east gate of the airbase but suddenly everything had changed. A strange light had been spotted far within the forest. Three patrolmen set out to investigate. In the pitch black, they headed along the network of paths that weaved amongst the vast maze of conifers. Under the cloak of the dark December night they walked deeper into the forest towards the source of the light.

'Look. There it is again. It's that way. Come on!' the first patrolman shouted and they gathered speed.

The light was so bright that they shielded their eyes as they edged forward to the clearing. It shone out in bright bursts and as they walked through the gap in the trees it lit up the forest revealing the huge spaceship. It sat silently, the ground around it scorched with the heat. Branches of nearby trees had been ripped from their trunks and were scattered on the ground where the ship had forced its way down through the canopy to crash land on the forest floor.

'Oh, my God. Is that what I think it is?' the first patrolman shouted. He took tentative steps towards to ship.

'Be careful Gary, we don't know what we are dealing with here,' his colleague called to him. He watched as the patrolman stepped nearer to the vehicle.

Gary's confidence began to grow the closer he got to the craft and he put his arm out and touched the metal of the ship, immediately pulling his hand away.

'Christ that's hot!' he yelled, 'There seems to be some kind of markings on the side,' he called back to the other two patrolmen who waited back in the wings. Gary pulled out a notebook from his pocket and began to draw the hieroglyphs that decorated the side of the ship. 'I wonder what they mean?' he mumbled to himself as he scribbled. The place was now in darkness and he tried to point his torch to the paper as he hurriedly drew the markings he saw. Dissatisfied with his first attempts he ripped the page from his notebook and began to draw them again.

'Come on Gary, we should go get help,' his friend called to him as he scanned the area around them with his eyes. A sudden flash of light revealed two figures standing behind the ship, dressed in grey space suits watching Gary as he wrote in his notebook. Their faces were obscured from view by the helmets that clung tightly to their heads. To the patrolman, they seemed to have some sort of device strapped to their backs - breathing apparatus perhaps?

The flash of light disappeared as quickly as it had come and they were plunged back into darkness save for their torchlight

'Gary! Watch out. I saw them. Aliens! Standing behind the craft! Let's get out of here and go back to the base!' he shouted and turned tail and began to hot foot it away from the clearing.

Another flash and Gary saw the figures as they were momentarily lit up. They stood motionless watching him. Were they planning on attacking him? Their spaceship had certainly given him a jolt like an electric shock when he had touched it. The shorter being's strange helmet had become dislodged and during the short bursts of light he could make out vague features. It looked almost human. Who were they? Were they friendly or should he be cautious? He raised his gun as a precaution. They weren't to know it wasn't loaded. Personnel weren't allowed to be armed when they left the base but these alien fuckers weren't to know that.

The forest plunged back into darkness and he called out to them, 'Who are you? Where do you come from?'

In the blackness, he shone his torch towards where they had been standing but they had gone. Vanished from sight.

A loud roar filled the air along with another flash of lights. The sound of animals in distress from across the fields echoed across to him, obviously disturbed by the noise. Then he heard the sound of a woman screaming. The whole area was in turmoil.

He didn't know where the aliens had gone, they could be about to jump him. He decided to run. His colleagues shouted at him and so in the darkness he made for their voices, heading back to the base. They would have to return in daylight.

June 2015

Claire lay awake for hours trying to make sense of what had happened that day. They had been sitting on the bench about to have their lunch when the men had appeared. It was just after the rain had stopped but the air had been fired with electric charge from the storm, it was shooting down forks of lightning around them. The humidity caused great swirls of mist to rise up from the ground as the moisture from the rain evaporated from the sodden forest floor. It was then that the men seemed to appear from within the mist.

Claire and Steve had stood up, wondering who they were. They looked official, wearing some sort of military uniforms. Maybe the area was out of bounds? But it can't have been, they were following a tourist trail. They had every right to be there. It was then that they realised the man walking closer to the spacecraft was armed. Steve whispered to her to stay still. They watched as the man touched the craft, acting as if it was real and not some cheap and nasty replica. He pulled his hand away as if the spaceship had burned him.

The electric storm continued to light up the sky every few minutes and they were able to watch as the man drew the pictures into his notebook. The whole situation felt unreal. Who were these men? Claire didn't think she could stay still much longer. She was scared. There was a gust of wind and her hood fell away from her face. She felt vulnerable now the man could see her features, maybe recognise her again. Steve whispered reassuring words to her but then the man pointed the gun at them and asked them who they were. Was he going to kill them? Then, an almighty crash of thunder set the animals into a commotion again over at the farm. Initially Claire had thought that the gun had been fired and she had just lost it and couldn't keep still any longer. She screamed. Steve grabbed her hand and they ran, jumped onto their bikes, and didn't stop until they reached the camp site.

They had gone straight across to the campsite office and Steve had asked if there had been any war games going on in the forest that day, paint ball type events but the woman on duty told him nothing like that ever took place in the forest. They told her what had happened but she eyed them with suspicion as if they were the threat. She obviously thought they were crazy.

The whole incident had felt so unreal that they began to wonder if they had dreamt it. They felt they would be ridiculed if they reported it to the Police. Claire was petrified that they might encounter the men again and persuaded Steve that they would go home the next morning.

Now as she lay in the van thinking about what had happened, a mad thought struck her. Had they been looking into the past? Had they been witnessing an event from 1980 - *the* event from 1980? The men had American accents, they were in uniform and one of the men shouted something about going back to the base. The more she thought about it the more she felt there may be some truth in it.

She finally managed to drift off to sleep and next morning she spoke to Steve about her ideas.

'But it can't be Claire. The guy was looking at the replica spaceship. If we were looking back to the past it would have been a real ship he would have seen.'

'Yes, I know. But what if it was the replica ship that they came across that night. What if they were in some sort of time loop or something?'

'But how would that work?'
'You're right, it's a mad idea. Come on, let's just pack up and go home.'

Debbie, the site owner watched as their camper van trundled out of the campsite. There was something troubling her about that young couple's story. She'd read a number of accounts about the UFO incident and their tale struck a chord. Something niggled in the back of her mind. She had taken a walk up to the clearing after they had come into the office. It was quiet there, no sign of any disturbance. Her fingers lightly touched the metal of the replica ship. It was cool to the touch. She shook her head and laughed to herself. These tourists have vivid imaginations! It was then that she had spotted the paper on the ground. She crouched down and picked it up. It was a page from a small notebook with some rough attempts of drawing the markings from the side of the spaceship. She frowned. Why can't these people take their rubbish with them? She popped it into her jeans pocket and headed back.

Next day back in the office after the couple had driven off she was kept busy most of the morning with new arrivals and paperwork. It was later that afternoon that she was able to steal away to her little sitting room for a quiet hour or so. Debbie sat down and stretched out her legs and sighed. She hoped she'd be able to have a snooze, especially as the noisy black helicopter that had been flying low over the forest these past few days seemed to have finally finished it manoeuvres but she knew it was unlikely that she'd sleep. She kept on thinking about the couple and their story. There was something deep within her memory about the UFO incident that she needed to recall. It was no good, she'd have to see what she could find out. She began pulling out various books from the bookcase, skimming through pages, searching for something that might give her a clue.

She had begun to give up hope when she came across a small booklet that she had purchased at a meeting that had taken place some years back in the local village hall. One of the men involved with the initial sighting had come over from America to give a talk to the many UFO story followers. He had new evidence he had said. Debbie had gone along but it had been a sell out and all the tickets had gone so all she could get was the booklet. She'd been so fed up that she'd not gone in for the talk she'd hardly looked at the book at the time.

She then remembered - she had been lucky to get a copy at all, as a strange thing happened after she'd bought the booklet. As she was leaving a tall man in dark glasses swung open the glass doors and walked in. She was about to tell him that he'd not get a ticket but he had pushed past her. So, she had stood outside the main door and watched as he went over to the guy selling the books, who stood up from his desk and backed away from the man. The man had then gathered up the rest of the booklets, threw them into a box and headed back to the door with them all. She had dashed down the steps and got out of sight until the man had driven off. So it was likely that she was one of the few people with a copy of this so called 'new evidence'. She opened it and began to read.

The ex-military man wrote how it was alleged that no photographic record of the event existed as it was claimed that all photos the men took at the time were over exposed. But some did actually survive. The whole incident was deemed to be such a mind- blowing enigma that it was ordered to be kept top secret. But he'd kept the photographs without the knowledge of the authorities but had never released them for public view. He had been too scared to show them in case he met an untimely death at the hands of the people who wanted to keep the whole thing quiet. He was now battling cancer so felt he had nothing to lose revealing all.

Debbie flicked through the pages and saw the photos of the patrolman's notebook. She gasped and felt in her pocket. Opening up the crumpled page she'd found in the clearing she compared it to the pictures of the notebook in the booklet. Surely this couldn't be from the same notebook after all these years? It must be a mistake. Then as she turned the page, a photograph jumped out at her and she felt as if her heart had stopped. Here was the new evidence. It was a photograph taken at the time by the patrolman who had stood back in the shadows. A photograph of the two aliens standing behind their ship. But not in spacesuits.

They were standing perfectly still in their grey waterproof trousers and grey waterproof jackets with their backpacks in place. One of them had a hood covering his features but the other's hood had fallen down revealing her face, white with fear.

It told how they were there one minute and then disappeared. Debbie knew where they had gone. She'd seen them drive out in their campervan early that morning. Her ears picked out the rumble of the helicopter in the distance and she felt an icy chill sweep through her veins. She put the booklet in the grate, struck a match and watched as it burnt away to nothing.

Steve and Claire were nearly home but had been sent on a diversion as the notice in the road had announced the main A road was closed. It was odd as they'd not seen any other traffic along the diverted route. Steve drove their little van along the dusty track following the signs.

'This is more like a footpath it's so narrow! Hope we don't meet anything coming the other way,' he said as they came to a tight bend and then found themselves face to face with a huge dumper truck. He gripped the wheel tightly and swung it round to avoid the truck before they plummeted over the edge of the quarry.

The black helicopter circled above the mangled camper van before flying away.

Heat

I feel the droplets of salty moisture slowly make their way down in between my breasts. My chemise clings to my skin as the heat increases. I hold my head high and look towards the buildings that skirt the Market Place. I will not let them see my fear.

The people jeer at me. I hear their shouts. Why do they hate me so? For all I have done was to heal the woman. Why do the men in their fancy clothes and their clever words look down on me? They pander to the physicians who have the mad notion that to take the life blood from people it will heal their ailments. Did I not cure the woman of her pain using the medicines that have been put here for us to use? The woods and the hedgerows supply our needs. It is Mother Nature who I worship, she looks out for us all. But the people of Bishop's Lynn attack me, tell me I consort with their Devil. He does not exist in my world.

I can feel the flames are growing higher now, soon they will consume my flesh. I must be brave. The Goddess will protect me as I return to her and the soil to grow once more.

'Witch,' I hear them cry. I spit at them and shout loudly my words. 'Threefold it shall return to you.'

I hear their laughter. They do not understand. Not yet. But they will, the law of the universe will play its final hand. You shall receive threefold that which you give.

I have never felt such heat. The smell of my burning flesh fills my lungs. The pain is becoming too hard to bear. I feel my heart thumping within my breast, getting faster and stronger. Faster still. My time has come to die. The sea of faces blur as I finally lose my body to the flames.

As my soul ascends high above the inferno, my heart continues to pump the molten blood around my body of fire. It rages with the anger of the Goddess until the fire within it bursts forth from my chest.

I look down and watch as my beating heart, blood red with fire and fury flies across the square and hits hard against the wall of the fine brick house.

I hear the people's cries and then there is silence as they watch the heart, my heart, bounce off the brickwork leaving my mark. A heart in red is carved into the building. The people gasp in disbelief. And then as if it had wings of its own, my heart heads out towards the river. The townsfolk listen in awe as the waters open, the waves of heat bubble in the river as my heart descends into the murky depths.

They stand quietly, unsure of what has happened. I watch as they look to each other for answers. Stunned, they slowly disperse as the remains of my body hangs limply on the stake as the water is thrown from buckets over my blackened and smouldering corpse.

It is time for me to go, but I shall return briefly as I wish to witness their fear and despair as the threefold returns. I shall watch as the fire consumes their buildings, their livelihood. I ask that no lives are taken but I will watch as they rush panic-stricken, trying to save their homes. I ask the Goddess if she shall save the brick building with my imprinted heart from the inferno. Let them remember me. Let not this madness happen again.

For I am a witch and I heal and wish you no harm.

The Whispering Wood

The click click of the needles invaded the silence as I finished the jumper I am making for my son. I checked the time. He should be back soon. He is collecting kindling from the wood. The wood where the wind whispers to those who listen. It is said it is full of ghosts but nobody knows who they once were. They don't want to give up their secrets easily.

The door slammed shut and Ernest stared at me, his face revealing his terror. I placed my knitting on the table and jumped up and rushed towards him.

'Ernest, whatever is wrong?' I asked, grabbing his hand in mine. He continued to gaze ahead, his emotions rendering him mute. 'Come, sit down,' I said.

I pulled his arm gently and guided him to the seat where he slumped down, slowing shaking his head from side to side. Holding onto his hand, I stroked his strong weather worn fingers. For all his outward looking strength, my boy was a gentle soul, he had been born with a kind heart and had been a great support when I lost his father to consumption. But then the war arrived and Ernest had been fired up like I had never seen before. He'd ran into the house, eyes ablaze with excitement as he told me he had joined the army along with his old school pals. I can still recall the pain I had felt in the pit of my stomach. I had already lost one man I had loved, I couldn't survive if my son was also taken from me.

But he was one of the lucky ones. He had returned from war but his kind heart had been emptied of all emotion except fear. I had been told stories of the trenches, that it had been hell for our young men, but my boy had returned with his own piece of hell snapped tight within his brain. I would hear his shouts in the night as his mind would awaken within his sleeping body, sending him visions of his horrific memories. He would call out into the darkness like a child for his mama. I would go to him, where he sat huddled in the corner of his room, his arms wrapped tightly around his legs as he attempted to make himself as small as he could manage. And all the while his quivering mouth emitting a whimper like an anguished dog. I will never forget that sound until the day I die. Over time the nightmares slowly eased but not before they had taken the life from him and for the past twenty years he had been an empty shell.

Although all that had been my boy seemed gone forever he had been left with a gift, or was it a curse? Maybe this was the reason for his current paralysis? Had he seen something new, something so terrible it had stuck him dumb? As the night terrors had eased he began to have visions, seemingly foretelling events before they occurred. He had seen the terrible starvation our people suffered after the end of the Great War. He knew how the influenza would take so many of our countrymen and so many across the western world. So many deaths. We were lucky, being so isolated, the disease never reached us and being forewarned by my son's premonition we stayed away completely from civilisation and we were spared.

The day Hitler became chancellor in 1933 Ernest had told me that it would lead to prosperity for the nation but it would be at a terrible cost to many innocents. I had asked him what he meant by this but he had shaken his head and told me it was better I didn't know. Buried deep in the east of the country we were shielded from a lot of the events as they unfolded but by 1938 we knew the prospect of another war was but a breath away. I prayed it wouldn't happen. Surely the world had learnt from the conflict in 1914 that more is lost than gained?

Life after the Great War had been difficult for many in our country but we had got by. Ernest had gone back to working the land. We were fortunate living amongst the trees and fields. The village was far enough away that we were not bothered by people. We kept to ourselves and Ernest liked it that way. I was the one who went to the stores for provisions.

The only person who would come to see us was Anna. She would visit most days, making her way to us through the woods that had skirted the west of the village for centuries. Ancient oaks stood deep within the forest, surrounding the crumbling old folly that stood derelict beneath the creaking boughs. Not many people ventured within the depths of the wood, too many tales of ghosts, demons and tree spirits kept most away. But Anna would tread her way carefully around the bracken and ferns and jump the fallen trunks like a graceful gazelle. Although in her late thirties, she was a child of the trees and her innocence had a healing effect on my boy. Before the war, she and Ernest had been sweethearts but when he returned he had told her that he did not want her anymore, that she should seek out a man who could be strong for her. She had smiled and looked into his troubled eyes, telling him she would wait for as long as it took. Even though she knew in her heart it would be an infinite wait she wouldn't entertain any other suitors and had kept herself pure. I knew his love for her was still buried deep within his tormented mind so if I couldn't manage to find a way inside his head today and discover what had triggered his latest fear I knew Anna would succeed where I failed.

I heard the latch of the gate and peered out of the window. Anna was making her way along the path, her dark hair shining in the sunlight. The wild flowers she had gathered hung their heads over the edge of her basket which was packed tight with butter and eggs from her father's small holding. We would trade their produce with our vegetables and the fruit harvest.

'Anna, welcome dear girl,' I greeted her with a kiss to her cheeks as she stood at the door. She saw the concern in my eyes.

'Etta, what is it? Is Ernest well today?'

I shook my head, 'Sadly no, his eyes are empty. I don't know what to do for him.' I began to cry. Anna placed her basket to the ground and swept me into her arms. My frail bones welcomed her embrace and I sobbed as she held me tight, stroking my back, whispering words of comfort.

A crash from the parlour startled us both and we turned to see Ernest standing in the doorway. He looked at Anna with great sadness.

'Anna. You must go.' Tears began to overflow onto his cheeks, 'You must go far away from here. I cannot bear it!' his mouth was contorted with distress. He rushed forward and grabbed at her arms and pulled her to him, 'Anna, Anna. What have they done to you. My God, if only I was stronger.'

'What is it Ernest? Come on my angel. Let us sit and talk. Tell me. Tell me what ails you. You ARE strong. With my love, I will help you become strong again.'

For a brief moment, I saw his eyes show a spark of the eighteen year old boy he had been in 1914 and slowly he began to open up and tell us the things he had seen in the whispering woods.

It was late when Anna left. Ernest had walked her to the gate and kissed her softly on the cheek. My boy was slowly returning.

We had arranged to meet up just before sunrise at the folly in three days time. Anna was going to try to get her father to believe Ernest's premonitions and journey with us.

We packed as much as we could carry into two small cases and we made our way into the woods. We both knew the dangers we would face but seeing the strength slowly return to Ernest gave me hope that we would survive. We heard voices in the distance and trod carefully as we walked through the bracken towards the old derelict building. We had to be careful, we couldn't assume it was Anna and her Father we could hear. Soldiers in Nazi uniform had been seen in the village a few days before, they would stop us if they knew where we were headed.

The folly came into view and Anna came running to us. Her father obviously troubled, was pacing backwards and forwards under the trees.

'Etta? Do you really believe it to be true...these visions that Ernest has....do you really believe him?'

I nodded, 'I do Otto. He was right about the influenza, and he knew the Fuehrer had started to secretly re-arm the country ten years ago. He knew he would transform the country but at great cost. We must go. He has seen what will become of us. We are not safe.'

He nodded, 'If you have such faith in him then I believe you Etta. Come Anna we must go quickly.'

We took the path towards the track that skirted the west side of the woods and dashed across to Otto's pickup truck that he had hidden away behind the bushes. He helped me into the seat beside him and Anna and Ernest clambered into the open load area behind. They pulled the sacking over themselves, hiding from view. Otto covered the hessian with turnips to try to disguise their shapes. We were lucky, the roads we took were empty for many miles and the further we travelled the more my stomach stopped churning with fear. We kept to the woodland tracks whenever we could and slept in barns and sheds and under the stars. It was a rough and frightening time but we finally reached the border and safety.

It was in my 70th year that I finally saw my Ernest marry his sweetheart. Anna had waited thirty-two years and looking at their smiling faces I knew they both thought it had been worth the wait. We had been in England for eight years. Everything Ernest had foretold had come true. The war had come as he had predicted but there had been one vision he had kept from us, the vision that had finally given him back his strength to fight for us and for the honour of his sweetheart. The Red Army had crossed into the east of Germany in 1944 and like a plague of locust had raped young and old. We heard that our village had been victim of these terrible crimes, the women being dragged into the woods, taken to the old folly and the Russian men had forced themselves upon them before killing them.

These terrible events took place in the wood where the wind whispers to those who listen. It is said it is full of ghosts but nobody knows who they once were. They don't want to give up their secrets easily but somehow on that day in 1938 they were able to cross the boundaries of time and forewarn my son.

The Bone Mill

She stood and watched as the colour slowly faded from his face. Her heart sounded loudly in her head as she waited to see if he would move. He'd been still for five minutes now. Five minutes since she smashed the shovel over his head. Her mind was awash with conflicting thoughts. Why had she gone this far? Why didn't she just accept that he was the bailiff and whatever he said was believed by the master. But the injustice of it all had made her see red. Why should they be victimised just because she wouldn't allow him to bed her? The blind fury took over again and she spat on his face.

'That's for all the suffering you've caused my brother Billy and me,' Annie said to the silent corpse of Tom Granger, 'Can't pester me now can ye?'

She wasn't going to degrade herself. They would find a way to survive. He'd laughed at her when she had told him they'd manage without his help. He had mocked her ideas of growing their own vegetables to help fill the cooking pot.

'You'll not get anything to grow in this barren soil girl. Why do you think these slums are still standing? The land's no good for 'owt but somewhere for low life like you to live,' he'd laughed... just before she had brought the shovel down on his head.

Suddenly the enormity of what she had done hit her and she began to shake. It had all happened so suddenly. He had turned up when she had been shovelling coal into a bucket for the range. It needed feeding more regularly this week, as the temperature had dropped. It was April but the wind had picked up since Sunday. It brought with it an icy chill from the east and as she stood lost in her thoughts, recalling the events, it blew the smoke of the smouldering bonfire into her eyes. The showers throughout the day had all but put it out.

She had been trying to clear away all the vegetation she and Billy had cut back ready to make room for the vegetable plot and she had begun burning it earlier that morning. Billy's overseer at the Bone Mill had promised to let him have some fertiliser that his work at the mill helped to produce. It would nourish the sandy soil and give them a better crop and hopefully make sure they would eat better than the winter just past. With Billy's accident, it had been a rough few months. As she felt droplets of rain fall onto her skin she sprang into action. She'd have to move Tom Granger's body out of sight and then would decide what to do.

Hitching up her petticoats, she placed her hands, strong from long days working the fields, onto his arms and dragged his body towards the coal shed. She'd keep him in there for now. She couldn't have Billy finding out.

She was just putting down the latch to the shed when she heard a voice. It was Liz. She stood in the yard and eyed Annie, with a look of understanding.

'You alright girl?' Liz said, her gaze flicking briefly towards the coal shed.

Annie pushed the wet tendrils of hair away from her rain sodden face, 'How long you be there Liz?'

'Long enough girl,' Liz folded her arms and gave the situation some thought. She'd known Annie and her brother Billy since they were babes. Their mother, Greta, had been her friend. She had passed on some five years now. A good woman Greta, honest and fair, but she wouldn't take injustice. What had been happening between Annie and Tom Granger had been unjust that was sure. Billy and Annie had fallen behind with the rent and Tom threatened to evict them. If left to Lord Munford to decide, he would more than likely give them a few weeks grace but if his bailiff evicted them he wouldn't argue. He left the tenancy issues to Tom Granger, he couldn't be doing with wasting his time on petty issues. So, Granger, in the knowledge that he could do almost as he will, had given Annie an option, an option she had refused. He hadn't been happy that one of the women in Rattle Row had refused his advances. That was how he'd got his sexual pleasures. He'd turn a blind eye to the late rent if they did as he wanted.

'How long he been pestering you Annie?'

'On and off since harvest time. It was a bad one as you know and then Billy scalded himself badly so couldn't earn a wage for a while. So Granger suggested an alternative to cash rent.'

'I don't blame you me ducks for holding back...but wouldn't it have been easier all round? Better than this outcome,' Liz's head nodded toward where his corpse now lay.

'What and get the clap like the others? Then where I be? I don't want to end up like Sophie Baxter. It got her bad. How do I pay rent then, if I get put away? What about Billy? His earnings up at the Bone Mill wouldn't cover the rent. No, we would have managed Liz. I've cleared all the brambles by the river's edge and Billy's cut the shrubs, it's given us some growing space in the yard. Once it's all burnt down, it'll give good soil to grow vegetables, that'll help us a fair bit.'

As the shower began to gain momentum Liz grabbed at Annie's hand, 'We best go see that he really is dead. Come me ducks, let's get this over with.'

The two women made their way to the coal shed. Annie's finger's fumbled with the latch and they went inside. The April shower drummed heavily on the tin roof and Annie began shivering again when she caught sight of Granger's body as it lay in the corner by the pile of coal.

Liz took off her shawl and put it around the young woman's shoulders, 'Come now Annie, we'll sort this out.'

'But I'll hang Liz. I'll hang for his murder,' Annie cried and fell to the floor.

What could she do? Billy would be back from the mill that evening and when he saw what she had done he wouldn't let her take the blame. She knew her brother too well. He had stood up for her since they'd been small, always there fighting her corner. So that was why she didn't tell him about Granger's advances and their troubles. Billy would have swung for her, that's for sure but now she had put him in that position herself. She couldn't, wouldn't allow it. Her astute mind whirled with a plan and she stood up and faced Liz.

'I'm going to get rid of the body Liz, so if you wish no part in this you best be on your way, I'll not have you getting caught up in my troubles.'

'I'm here to stay my girl. But get rid of his body? How you going to do that?'

'I'll burn it on the bonfire. If I get some reeds from the river it will get the fire going again. I'll burn the bastard, that's what I'll do!'

Annie glanced across at Billy as he ate his supper. He'd caught a couple of rabbits the night before and she'd made a stew that would last them a good few days. She hoped her eyes wouldn't give away her anguish. She had managed to convince him all was well when she had stopped him going to get more coal from the shed earlier. She'd pushed him back down on the seat telling him he'd worked hard enough that day.

She watched as he scooped up the last of the meat juices with a hunk of crust and wiped his mouth with the back of his hand.

'That was right tasty Annie.'

'If you'd not got the meat it would have been veg broth again, so it be thanks to you too Billy,' Annie said and gathered up the dishes and took them through to the scullery. She tied the apron around her waist and leant against the draining board as her mind pondered on a solution to her troubles. She started to scrape the rabbit bones into the bone pot ready to take up to the Mill. Most of the residents from the cottages in Rattle Row took their old food bones up to the mill where they were boiled up by Billy and the other workers to rid them of the marrow so they were then ready for grinding. They got a few coins for them so it was worth the mile walk alongside the river.

Annie lifted the heavy kettle from the range and poured the steaming water over the greasy plates and lost in her thoughts she began the task of washing up. She had been grateful for Liz's help earlier. They had got the fire burning again despite the rain and had dragged Tom Granger's body onto the pyre. The smell of burning flesh had made them retch but they were used to disgusting smells. Up at the mill the whale bones were boiled and then ground ready to make the fertiliser and when the wind came from the west the stench could be overpowering at times.

The fire had done its best to rid Annie of the evidence of her crime, but the showers had turned heavy and extinguished the bonfire so now she still had his bones to dispose of. They'd buried them under the elder tree but then Annie had worried that a fox might dig them up so had shoved them under the pile of coal for now until she could make up her mind what to do with them. She wiped the last plate dry and her eyes caught sight of the bone pot. Of course! Why didn't she think of that before!

Next day up at the mill they had weighed the bag of bones she had taken along to them.

Billy had been on site working and had looked across and winked at her. To him the joke had been that she had been handing over the bones from the rabbits he had poached from Lord Munford's estate. He didn't realise he was about to boil down the bailiff's bones too.

'Here Billy, you ready for some more?' Annie asked and tipped the bones from the bag into the boiling liquid, shielding the evidence from view. No-one had seen them, no-one would ever know there had been human bones amongst them.

Billy's guvnor had handed her the coins with a smile. She had done well and now had 4d in her pocket.

'Here you are Annie love. Every little helps to make good fertiliser. Did Billy tell ye that I can give you some for that vegetable patch you be digging? These here bones you've brought along will be having your vegetable patch growing a treat in no time.'

She walked alongside the river, heading back home with a spring in her step. She smiled to herself. It looked as if she was going to get some help with the vegetable plot from Tom Granger after all.

About the author

Jan Foster-Bartlett rekindled her love for creative writing when she relocated to her maternal grandmother's roots of rural Norfolk.

Voices in the wood and other tales was first published on kindle in 2013. This printed version is a mix of the majority from that earlier publication combined with stories taken from Jan's other short story book on Kindle – The Black Horse ghost. The Legacy was previously published in 2011 by oakmagic publications as part of an anthology of Norfolk Tales. Jan's novel, Echoes at the Abbey, a supernatural story with a hint of history and romance, was published in 2014 and the sequel, Revenge at Greysmead will be published Spring 2018.

Printed in Great Britain
by Amazon